The Preacher's
First Murder

K.P. Gresham

First Book in the
Preacher Matt Hayden Mystery Series

The Preacher's First Murder
A Pastor Matt Hayden Mystery

This is a work of fiction. Characters, places and events
are the product of the author's imagination or are used
fictitiously and are not to be construed as real.
Any resemblance to events, locales, organizations, or persons,
living or dead, is entirely coincidental.

Cover Design by Renee Barratt, www.TheCoverCounts.com
Formatting by www.polgarusstudio.com

Paperback ISBN: 978-0-9967002-0-7
E-book ISBN: 978-0-9967002-1-4

Printed in the United States of America

First Print Edition

Library of Congress Control Number: 2016931609

*This is dedicated to my mom and dad up there in heaven, and
my husband, Kevin, and daughter, Bethany
here on earth.*

Thank you, God, for blessing me beyond measure.

Table of Contents

Chapter One
The Angel on Fire

Pastor Matt Hayden stared at the wad of Benjamin Franklin faces in his hand. Two thousand dollars cash. He fought to control the jolt of surprise at seeing that much money. He remembered another time, another lifetime . . . seven years ago when he was a different person with a different name—an undercover cop of twenty-five by the name of Mike Hogan.

"Make it happen, man."

Michael Hogan Jr. played his part, scratching at his dirty sun-bleached hair, readjusting the sunglasses hiding any expression in his blue eyes. After three months on this sting, he still had to finish it. He took a wad of hundred-dollar bills from his filthy jeans pocket, considered them carefully, then traded them for the bag of white powder in the hooded teenager's hand. A chilly morning breeze whipped across Biscayne Bay and whirled in the corner of shipping crates where he and the gang leader hid from view. Afraid the bag would blow away,

Mike tucked it in his pocket, refusing to look around to see if the not-so-asleep bum had caught the transaction on the camera hidden in his coat.

Although Mike knew it was coming, the sudden charge of police officers around the crates caught him by surprise. They tackled the hooded banger and threw a few punches as the teenager kicked hard, trying to break free.

It was then that Mike saw the plain-clothes cop approaching down the dock. It was his father, Captain Michael Hogan Sr., who was in charge of the bust. The father and son looked at each other across the pier, sharing a split second of pride.

Suddenly a shot rang out, and the look of pride on Michael Sr.'s face froze. He clutched at his chest. When he pulled his hand away, it was soiled with blood.

"Dad!" Mike started to run for him.

That's when he saw Skimmer, the gang's lookout, peering over the dock from a speedboat. His black face turned blacker with rage.

"You're a sonuvabitch cop!" Skimmer raised his gun.

Another blast rent the air and Skimmer's weapon flew out of his hand. The next explosion got him right between the eyes. Two cops converged on the boat.

Mike continued to run until he reached his father's side. He slid to his knees, grabbing for his father's hand.

"Tipped off," Michael Sr. rasped out.

"Don't talk, Dad. You need your strength." Mike tried not to stare at the blood that spurted from his father's chest at each breath.

"Too late." His dad shook his head. "Knew he wanted to get me. Shoulda told you."

"You can tell me later." Mike held his dad's hand tighter.

The next breath rattled in his father's chest. "I love you, son."

"I love you too, Dad." Mike choked off a sob as his dad's eyes went lifeless.

"You all right, Preacher?" James W. Novak's voice broke into Matt's memories.

"That's a lot of money, James W." Matt forced himself back to the present. He wasn't in Florida, working the drug scene of Miami's harbors. He was in Wilks, Texas, plying his new trade of prayer and peace, talking with the sheriff in the church parking lot. He slammed the door of his Ford Tempo closed and leaned against its frame.

"Mamma's that kind of person, Preacher." James W. Novak was a large man. His khaki sheriff's uniform pulled at the buttons on his round chest. "Everybody knows this heap you're drivin' ain't gonna make it much longer, and everybody knows you ain't got a down payment. When Miss Olivia sees somethin' that needs doing, she does it. She considers it her duty."

James W. eyed the preacher carefully. Though the January Texas sun was warm, it didn't warrant the sweat that now beaded on the new pastor's brow. The preacher was six foot anyway, and had an athletic build. He didn't look like the sickly type. "You eaten today, Preacher?"

"What exactly—" Matt held up the money, "—is my duty in return for this?"

James W. chuckled. "You're never sure exactly what Miss Olivia has on her mind."

Matt swallowed hard. He did need a down payment for a car, and he didn't have a dime to his name. Right was right, however, and strings were strings. Being beholden to the richest person in Wilks seemed like a whole lotta strings and not a whole lotta right. He stuffed the money into James W.'s shirt pocket. "But I'll let you buy lunch." He grinned.

"How 'bout Callie Mae's Cafe?"

"Sounds good. On the way I have a letter to mail at the post office."

The two men fell into a friendly amble as they crossed the Colorado River Bridge separating Grace Lutheran Church from the rest of Wilks. Matt had taken the call to the small rural town only six weeks earlier. With the rush of services for the Advent and Christmas seasons, he hadn't had much time to socialize.

As he reached the far riverbank, Matt forced himself to concentrate on the chatter of birds overhead, probably snowbirds down from the north for the winter. He'd chosen this docile community for a purpose. He wanted to block out everything that reminded him of Miami—its crime, its violence, its cemeteries. Yet the mere sight of cash had taken him back to that moment of his father being shot.

Maybe he should've joined a monastery like his brother had mockingly suggested. Monks weren't reputed to carry a lot of cash.

The pastor and the sheriff approached a battered two-story

brick structure that marked the start of commercial buildings at the tree-lined bank, and they turned to cross Mason Street. Even the new preacher had learned the unspoken rule about not walking on the same side of the street as the building owned by That Woman.

This time, however, the crossing was not the routine passage.

"James W.!" The female voice that called to the sheriff was rich and husky.

Matt had never heard her before. In fact he had only seen her from across the river. Nevertheless, he knew it was Her. The Angel by Day, Devil by Night. The woman his female parishioners talked of in hushed tones, indignant that an establishment of her sort stood so close to the church.

"You need somethin', Angie?" James W. walked to where she stood at the door of her "restaurant," the Fire and Ice House.

"You seen Mamma?" Angel O'Day's striking face was worried. She looked at James W. hopefully.

Matt wasn't sure whether to watch the exchange between the two or avert his eyes. Her long red hair flamed about her like something the angel Gabriel himself would unleash in the final battle. A simple look at her sent a man's heart racing.

Though he was a man of God, Matt Hayden was still a man.

"It's her walk time, ain't it?" James W. asked.

"Yeah. Shadow's with her. I guess I shouldn't be worried."

"He's more person than dog, that's for sure." James W. said. "Besides, you know Wilks. Anyone in this town'd take care of your mamma if they saw her headin' for trouble."

She didn't look convinced. "You had lunch?" she asked.

James W. cleared his throat and cast a sideways glance at Matt. As if only now realizing that the preacher stood there, Angie's head went up in defiant pride and her gaze narrowed. "I didn't realize," she said, her voice lowering to a simmer. "Y'all wouldn't be interested."

"Yes, we would." Matt heard the words, then realized in surprise that he was the one who had spoken them.

James W. grinned. "She's got the best red beans and rice in town." He looked at Angie. "It's red beans and rice on Saturdays, right?"

She refused to answer but turned her back on them and walked into the restaurant.

Matt was pretty sure he heard her mutter something about his clerical collar not fitting through the door. He gave the sheriff a questioning look. "Maybe—"

"She'll say you chickened out." James W. grinned.

"I'm not chickening out," Matt said, knowing full well that he was indeed.

"If you say so, preacher. After you." The sheriff gestured.

The Fire and Ice House was indeed an old converted fire station. Matt's first impression of the place was that it was dark, but then he realized that was more a result of the sudden departure of the bright Texas sun outside. The bar was on the left. Christmas lights twinkled beneath the liquor rack that surrounded the dark wood counter. Matt suspected they were a year-round fixture, not a leftover from the recent holidays.

The place smelled of cigarettes and Clorox bleach.

He followed the sheriff to a line of booths that separated the pool tables from the lounge. James W. slid into the nearest one as Patsy Cline's sultry voice crooned from the neon jukebox at the bar's edge.

"Shiner, Sheriff?" Angie came up to the table, a dish towel slung over her shoulder.

"Now, you know I'm on duty, Angie darlin'." The graying, sharp-eyed Czech smiled. "I'll take a Dr. Pepper." His gaze reverted to the old twenty-inch RCA tube TV hung above the bar.

"*Representative James W. Novak Jr., of Wilks, Texas, met with the Lone Star State's retiring Governor Burr this morning following Novak's announcement yesterday that he is running for the soon-to-be-empty seat.*" The blonde beauty of Austin's NBC affiliate announced from the broadcast desk, while a photograph of a young, sharp-eyed, red-haired man was positioned in the screen's corner.

Angie grinned at the screen. "Mighty proud of Jimmy Jr., Sheriff?"

Sheriff James W. Novak Sr. sat straighter in the booth and grinned. "Two stints as state representative, and already goin' for governor? You'd better believe I'm proud, little lady."

"Mamma took a real interest in that speech of his yesterday," Angie went on. "Kept callin' him J.J., though. Jimmy ain't never been called J.J., has he?"

The sheriff shrugged his shoulders. "You know Maeve."

A shadow of concern passed over Angie's face, then it was

gone. She turned to Matt. "Want a beer?" Angie asked, finally acknowledging that he sat across the booth from James W.

Matt shook his head, making sure his smile was in place. "Too early for me. Just tea, thanks."

Angie sniffed, then left to fetch the drinks.

"Maeve is her mother, I take it," Matt said.

"Alzheimer's." James W. nodded. "Noticed it about five years ago when she couldn't remember her mix for Bloody Marys." He chuckled. "That woman could pour a drink."

"Now?"

"Angie took over runnin' the place seven years ago. Maeve's been turnin' back the clock ever since then. Must think she's in her twenties now. Most of the time she thinks Angie's one of the girls from Miss Lida's."

"Miss Lida's?"

"That was what we called Wilks' house of ill-repute, Preacher," James W. said with a grin. "Maeve was the bartender there."

"I see." Matt wasn't sure he saw at all. James W. had a wicked sense of humor. He couldn't tell from the twinkle in the man's eye if bartending was the only service Maeve had provided at Miss Lida's.

Angie returned. She placed an opened bottle of Dr. Pepper in front of James W., then, with a thud, set a red tea glass in front of Matt. As she poured from the pitcher into his cup, the tea slurped over the side and spilled onto the table. She didn't bother mopping up the mess but flipped open her order book.

"Makes a hornet look cuddly, don't she?" James W. winked.

Matt shrugged, not knowing whether Angie enjoyed James W.'s teasing.

"Don't take it personal, Preacher. She don't cotton much to church folk." James W. slipped a pack of cigarettes from his pocket and shook out the last one. "I'll have the special."

Looking as if the asking would cause her to spit, Angie turned to Matt. "What'll it be, preacher man?"

Angie O'Day looked to be a formidable foe. Not that Matt considered her as such, but it was obvious she did. Her eyes, brown with flecks of gold, were angry and defensive.

"So you know who I am." Matt swallowed his moment of panic and smiled.

"Live next to you, don't I?" she asked sharply.

"Sorry I haven't gotten over here earlier." He smiled. "Moving in the day before Thanksgiving put me in a bind for getting settled until after Christmas."

Angie shrugged. "Whatever. You here to talk or to eat?"

"I'll have the special, I guess."

"You sure?" Her smirk was a challenge. "We've got burgers and fries, too."

"But your special is the red beans and rice. Right?"

"It's good ole' Texas food. You're a Yankee, ain't you?"

"I'm from Florida."

Angie rolled her eyes as if to say that was the same thing, but Matt persisted. "Red beans and rice'll be fine."

"Two specials!" She called into the kitchen as a short old woman was putting an order up at the window. The graying cook still had a youthful glint in her eye, but that was all her face hinted that she had once been young. The woman glanced at the preacher sitting at the booth, and the glint in her eye turned lethal.

Matt had not gotten such a cold reception in a long time. Usually his collar brought him at least a nod and maybe even a handshake.

Of course, it had been long a time since he'd walked into a house of ill repute.

"Hey, James W., Pastor Hayden, what a surprise." Matt looked up to find Ernie Masterson sitting at the bar. The Sinclair Station owner was positively grinning. Inwardly Matt groaned.

Ernie showed up to church every Sunday, Matt knew. He also knew that Ernie's Sunday morning hangovers caused the man to stick cotton in his ears to keep the pain from listening to Matt's sermons at bay. Though he would admit it to no one, Matt's decision to read the Gospel lesson from the center aisle, right next to where Ernie sat, had been inspired by Ernie's grimace.

Ernie Masterson stood up from his stool and slid in next to James W. He motioned to Angie for another beer.

"Heard you were askin' after your mother," Ernie said when she brought it over.

Angie looked up sharply. Matt noted her belligerent eyes immediately filled with interest. "You heard right."

"Saw her just before lunch. Headin' towards the square." Ernie downed half the beer in one long drink.

"Where to?"

Ernie belched. "I was pullin' Henry Jacobs' car out of the

garage. Oil change. Almost ran her over as she crossed the driveway."

"Was Shadow with her?"

"Like always," he said.

"When?" James W. asked.

"Musta been about 11:30," Ernie answered. "Before I came over for lunch."

"Dorothy Jo!" Angie called back to the kitchen. The cook's wrinkled face appeared at the window. "Ernie saw Mamma across the square. She gets lost over there. I'm gonna go find her."

Dorothy Jo nodded. "I'll watch the place."

"I'm headin' back to the garage." Ernie pulled himself to his feet. "Gotta work on Miss Olivia's car this afternoon," he said. His eyes danced in Matt's direction. He walked out of the bar, letting the screen door slam behind him.

The sheriff looked at the pastor and shook his head. Ernie's chuckle had been low and, Matt thought, sounded a little threatening.

Angie untied her denim apron and tossed it on a stool. As she headed around the bar toward the front door, she looked slyly at Matt Hayden.

"Ernie's got a mouth like Niagara Falls and he's gonna be workin' on Miss Olivia's car this afternoon." She paused at the front door. "Miss Olivia ain't gonna like hearin' about your bein' in my place, Preacher. Must admit, I wasn't too happy about it myself. But now . . ." Angie grinned. "Stop by some time in the evenin', preacher man. I charge a little more, but it's definitely worth your while."

***

Ernie Masterson walked across Mason Street to his Sinclair Station. Too bad he had to work on Miss Olivia's car this afternoon. He could've used another beer or two, and would've enjoyed watching the preacher try to eat Dorothy Jo's red beans and rice without hacking on the heat.

Ernie had to tow the line with Miss Olivia, though. She'd made sounds lately that she didn't care for how he treated Pearl, his wife. Apparently Miss Olivia had forgotten all the secrets Ernie knew about her past. He'd need to find some fresh dirt on the Wilks-Novak clan to regain his control over the matriarch.

After all, Jimmy Jr. Novak was running for governor.

"There you are," Pearl Masterson said when he walked through the station door. "You know today I fold bulletins with Miss Olivia over at the church."

"Hell, Pearl, I was just across the street at Angie's. I would've seen her if she drove up."

Pearl was a slight woman, with an even slighter chin. She rarely spoke harshly to her husband. That had taken years of training on his part, and he didn't care for the times when she forgot the lesson.

"Don't you want to ask me if Bo was working today?" Ernie's jab hit the mark. He watched his wife shrink away from him as if he'd slapped her. The rumors about Pearl and the bartender were beginning to take hold. He considered it had been one of his better ideas to start them.

"I'm going up to get my purse." She closed the cash register's drawer.

At that moment, Ernie heard a car pull up to one of the garage's repair bays. Ignoring the sound, he stayed put. He had one more topic to cover with his wife.

"Have you seen Maeve O'Day anywheres while I was gone?" Ernie asked as Pearl started up the stairs to their apartment.

"Actually, yes I did." She stopped. "I was walking back from the Courthouse so I could cover your lunch. Why?"

"Angie's lookin' for her. James W. and that new preacher are over there having lunch. They was talking about it."

"Reverend Hayden is at Angie's Fire and Ice House?" Pearl looked stunned.

Ernie grinned. Mission accomplished. Pearl was sure to tell Miss Olivia about the preacher's transgression, and then all hell would break loose.

"Yep," he replied. "Angie sure was paying him a lot of attention."

He could see Pearl was trying to decide exactly how much of what he said was true, and how much was his usual skank.

It wasn't right, a wife questioning his every word.

"Well, Shadow was with her. I'm sure she'll be fine." Pearl started up the stairs.

Another thought struck Ernie. "Was Maeve talkin' funny about anything?"

Pearl sighed. "She lives in a different world, Ernie. We shouldn't make fun of her."

"What did she say?"

"Oh, she was looking for somebody called J.J. I told her I don't know any J.J."

"J.J.?" Ernie's mind was a little slower than it used to be, he'd admit that. But now he was beginning to remember when there *had been* a J.J. in Wilks, Texas.

"She said he was a handsome guy with red hair. And had a way of talking that made her smile all the way down to her toes."

"You don't say." Ernie stood for a moment, taking it all in.

"Listen, honey, I'm sorry I was so mean to you when you came in. It's just you know Miss Olivia. She hates to be kept waiting."

Ernie decided to be nice. He was having too good a day to be forced to watch Pearl sulk for the rest of it. "She does indeed."

A relieved look came over Pearl's face. "Thanks, honey." She started back up the stairs. "I think I heard a car drive up to the garage."

"Yeah, yeah."

Ernie turned to go into the mechanic's shop. As he reached the door, however, he heard a car's tires screech out of the driveway.

What the hell? Ernie wondered. Just as well, he decided. He had to take a leak before Miss Olivia arrived.

Chapter Two
Welcome to Wilks, Preacher

The mid-afternoon sun peeked through the garage door windows of the Fire and Ice House. Warm enough to open them up and air out the place, Angie figured. She pulled hard on the rope and the doors squeaked as they rolled on their tracks, almost drowning out the phone when it began to ring.

Dorothy Jo appeared at the pass-through window. "That was James W. He's on his way over."

Angie nodded. "Thanks."

Mamma.

Angie automatically cast a look out the front doors of the Ice House. The warmth of the sunlit street enticed the Yeck brothers into moving their domino game out on the sidewalk. She helped them with their chairs, then glanced back to the street. The sun was bright enough to make her squint, she thought with relief. At least her mamma wasn't missing from home on a rainy day.

The Fire and Ice House was indeed Wilks' old fire station.

When Maeve O'Day bought the place, she'd converted the private quarters upstairs into a two-bedroom apartment for her and her daughter.

The Fire and Ice House was the only home Angie ever remembered.

She looked up and down Mason Street. To the right was the Colorado River, then Grace Lutheran. To the left and across the street was Ernie Masterson's Sinclair Station. Sinclair gasoline had long ago gone out of business in Texas, but Ernie had kept the green dinosaur sign on his building, and everyone still called his garage the Sinclair Station.

She waved at friends who looked her in the eye and smiled. She cast stoic glances toward foes who would rather die than acknowledge her presence. She saw cats prowling for their next meal and flocks of birds practicing for their spring migration back up north.

She didn't see a black dog with the body of a German shepherd and the face of a bloodhound who answered to the name of Shadow. She didn't see Maeve O'Day.

James W. pulled around the corner and parked his quad cab in the fire zone in front of Angie's restaurant.

"I didn't find her, James W." Angie glanced in frustration at her watch. "It's been three hours now."

James W. tapped his steering wheel, then nodded. "Guess I'd better get the boys out," he said, referring to his deputies.

Angie felt the relief come over her like a spring rain. "Thank God."

"Get that from your visitor this noon?" James W. smirked.

No, she thought. The only thing she'd gotten from that preacher man invading her territory had been a jolt of surprise at how good he'd looked. His hair was shades of light brown, with golden streaks that women paid good money to beauticians to create. His eyes were blue, a deep blue that looked through you. Not the kind of looks that Ernie Masterson gave that stopped at her bust line. No, the pastor's eyes looked deeper, into her very soul. If he were any other man, Angie would like to get to know him better.

For thirty-five years she'd been waiting for a man to stir her like that. The devil was handing her a wicked joke when he'd put that face on a preacher man.

Shaking off the image, Angie growled. "The man's a fool if he thinks he can get away with comin' in here. Can hardly wait to hear what your wife is gonna have to say about that."

"She lets me go in your place without a gripe."

"She thinks you're tryin' to close me down on a health violation." Angie looked at him pointedly. "Which you would do in a New York minute if I gave you reason."

"That's one of the things I like about you and me, Angie. We understand each other."

"It took all my self-control not to kick that man out of my place today. Hell, I was thrown out of his place. Turnabout is fair play."

"Why didn't you?"

"'Cuz I'm more Christian than that."

James W. laughed, then turned serious. "Look, little lady, this thing about your mamma goin' missing. We can't be doing this kind of thing all the time. Her condition is only goin' to get worse."

Angie bowed her head. "I know."

"Now, you've been a good daughter to that woman. Stood by her and given her the best you could. But you gotta start thinking about puttin' her in a place."

"A place?" Angie's eyes flashed.

"Don't you pull that Irish temper on me, young lady. I like you. Can't seem to help it. Bothers the hell out of me sometimes. Someone's got to tell you straight. She's getting where she don't know you anyhow, and I can't be putting out a search team every time she goes missing."

Angie nodded. She didn't agree with him, but she did understand. James W. had always been honest with her. And fair. Which was more than she could say for his mother.

"I'll think about it," she mumbled.

Knowing he had won a major victory, he put his truck in gear. Getting Angie O'Day to listen to something she didn't want to hear didn't happen very often. "I'll be in touch. Stay around your place," he ordered. "I need to know where to find you. Besides, chances are that dog of yours'll bring her home anyways."

"I hope you're right," Angie said. She watched James W. pull away from the curb and then do a U-turn to head back to the municipal building. "But I don't think you are." She sighed and walked back into her restaurant.

***

Elsbeth Novak folded the last of the bulletins for Grace Lutheran's Sunday services. "Her mother was a whore. And so is Angie O'Day." Elsbeth, wife to Sheriff James W. Novak, was squeezed into the mismatched brown upholstered chair at the desk's end. Grace's small church office was growing cold, the setting January sun only a hint of pink outside the single tall-paned window. The three women who made up the Saturday afternoon bulletin-folding committee talked heatedly, as if that alone would keep them warm. The cold gaze of the frailest and oldest of the three women spoke volumes. She believed the statement was indeed true.

"Whether she's a prostitute or not, a preacher shouldn't be seen in the company of a woman of that reputation." Miss Olivia Wilks-Novak was Elsbeth's mother-in-law and the last of the Wilks family for which the small Texas town was named. She sat behind the desk. "It's bad enough my son goes over there."

Pearl Masterson, the final member of Grace's folding committee, licked her thumb and inserted the announcement sheet into the bulletin handed her by Elsbeth. "Ernie heard it at lunch. Her mother is missing and your son is the sheriff, Miss Olivia." Pearl sat across from Miss Olivia and secured the middle of the four-page bulletin with one frugal staple. She set the finished project on the lone file cabinet in the room.

The file cabinet was kept locked, to the chagrin of the Saturday volunteers.

"That doesn't explain the minister's being over at that whorehouse today!" Elsbeth Novak huffed through her plump cheeks. "We'll ship him right back to the synod if that's what he has in mind."

"Good afternoon, ladies."

The quiet baritone voice of Reverend Matt Hayden caused an immediate hush in the whitewashed office. He leaned against the vestibule door, his blue eyes a study in diplomacy.

"Reverend," the three women murmured. Pearl Masterson smiled as best she could despite her chinless countenance. "We've finished folding."

"Bless your work." The pastor forced his smile to remain gracious. He'd heard every one of their remarks as he'd closed up the sanctuary after making sure all was in place for Sunday's festival of the Epiphany.

Pearl looked at her watch and stood, clutching a crocheted sweater about her thin shoulders. "Have to get dinner on. Miss Olivia, may I give you a ride since Ernie's working on your car?"

"Won't be necessary," a male voice called from behind the preacher. Ernie Masterson appeared in the doorway. "Thought I'd bring your car over, Miss Olivia, since it was done."

"That's kind of you," Miss Olivia allowed. She leaned heavily on her cane as she pulled her frail body from the chair.

"No problem." Ernie nodded. "I took the liberty of cleanin' your interior while it was in the garage. You shouldn't let your dog travel in the car."

Miss Olivia grunted. "Blanco enjoys his rides."

"Yes ma'am," Ernie said. "But that long black hair showed up somethin' fierce on your tan interior."

She looked at him a long moment. "I appreciate your help."

"I knew you would." Ernie donned his hat. "Pearl, you ready to fix me up some supper?"

"Yes, Ernie," the quiet woman said and obediently followed her husband out of the room.

Miss Olivia watched them go, turned and gave a pointed look toward Elsbeth. After a brief smile at the preacher, Miss Olivia shuffled from the room.

Matt noted with disdain that he'd been left to deal with Elsbeth Novak alone.

Or rather, she had been left to deal with him.

Elsbeth didn't take long to get to the point, he noted. "I understand you were over at That Woman's place for lunch today, Pastor Hayden." The imperious woman followed Matt into the vestibule.

Matt stacked the last of the three hundred bulletins on the carved oak squire's table. "The food tasted pretty good," he offered.

"It's bad enough my husband goes over there—though that's because he's trying to close her down." Elsbeth Novak frowned. "I'm telling him to put a stop to that today. James W. can't be worrying about liquor permits now," she said firmly. "You heard about Jimmy, Jr., running for governor?"

Matt smiled. "I saw it on the news last night. You must be very proud of your son, Mrs. Novak."

"I'm talking about your behavior, Reverend Hayden." Elsbeth Novak's eyes narrowed to a simmering stare. "I don't care if that girl's mother is missing. That old woman's got too many cobwebs in the attic, anyway."

"I believe she has Alzheimer's, Mrs. Novak."

Elsbeth's puffy face reddened, clashing vividly with her severe brown hairdo. "You're new around here, Preacher, and someone needs to tell you what's what."

"I see." Matt Hayden gave thanks the church was deserted except for him and his overbearing parishioner. Her voice raised to a sharp timbre and echoed off the linoleum floor into the hollow steeple above.

"Might as well tell you straight out. Maeve O'Day was a prostitute over at Miss Lida's Rose Hotel on the north side of town. Before Sheriff Danny Don Dube closed it down, anyway. That girl Angie O'Day is the product of a whore's paycheck."

Matt shifted uncomfortably. The story had been suggested to him before, but this was the first someone had told it to him outright.

"Angie's picked up right where her mamma left off. She has an ex-con—a murderer, no less!—come in and run things for her while she tends to her business upstairs."

Matt Hayden put his hands in his pockets. "That's a pretty strong statement, Mrs. Novak."

"All the more reason you should know your facts before going over there again."

"I see." Matt felt his anger flare, but squelched it. "I thank you for the warning." He turned off the interior lights and grabbed his jacket from the coat hook by the front door.

"Warning?" Elsbeth Novak echoed. "Pastor Hayden, you can do anything you want. I want you to know the facts, is all." She pulled a scarf over her ears against the cool night air while

Matt held the door for her. She smiled triumphantly. Her message had been received.

Her face puckered as she looked in the direction of the Colorado River and the infamous house beyond. "See that man? The one with the pony tail?"

Matt squinted through the dusk at the Fire and Ice House.

"That's her pimp. Imagine! That going on right next to the church!" Elsbeth sniffed and held out her hand for assistance down the ten cement stairs of Grace Lutheran. "I expect you to reconsider your patronage of that establishment, Preacher," she said, taking his arm.

Matt helped her into her white Oldsmobile and watched her pull away. Or else, he finished for her.

She drove off, leaving a trail of dust and distaste.

Matt looked up to the sky, from whence came his strength, he reminded himself. The peach sunset on the horizon melded into light and then dark blue as his eyes trailed up toward the heavens. The night was clear. Already a star shimmered against the darkest of the blue. The limestone steeple of Grace Lutheran reached far and up, the cross on its tip seemingly touching the twinkle of the planet Venus in the northern sky.

A breathtaking night, to be sure. Matt smiled. The Lord was cooking up a masterpiece.

Matt crossed the parking lot and headed for the small break in the bushes that marked the sidewalk to his new home. He zipped up his windbreaker against the chilly night and breathed deeply of the fresh, crisp country air—nothing like the smell of fish rot near Miami's docks where he'd grown up. Then a very different, very familiar scent caught in his nostrils.

Blood.

Fresh, wet, acrid blood that smelled of crime and violence and evil.

He turned toward the smell, knowing there would be a lot of it when he found it. Instinct brought the hair up on the back of his neck. He'd spent too much time as an undercover cop not to know danger.

Matt turned to the left, the direction from which the breeze brought the metallic smell of blood.

Then he heard the moan. The low moan of pain. It didn't sound human.

Matt squinted in the waning light and followed his nose to a grouping of pampas grass at the edge of the church's parking lot.

The whimpering was louder now. More heart wrenching. Finally, he saw the dark form huddled into a ball near the wheat-like plumes of grass.

The dog was a large one, the shape and coloring of a German shepherd with the face of a bloodhound. Tight around its neck was a leather leash, and the dog was almost choking with it. "Take it easy, boy," Matt said softly as the dog raised its head to look at him.

Matt loosened the leash. The dog's head fairly dropped to the ground with relief. Matt leaned over to pet the animal.

His hand touched sticky, wet fur.

He pushed back the weight of the pampas grass, allowing the parking lot light to shine on the dog. Bile belched up the back of the preacher's throat.

The dog was drenched in blood.

Chapter Three
Shadow

Bobby Peveto, or Bo as he was known, was a man with a past. He wore black because it suited him to remember his dark beginnings. He wore a ponytail because it appealed to the hippie he had once been. He wore a scar across his nose and cheek because a man in prison chose him to be a boy-toy and Bo begged to differ.

Few knew his real name because that was the way he wanted it. He figured if a person knew your name, they could look you up on the computer or get your name from prison files. His boss knew his name, and that made his paperwork square with the IRS. His parole officer knew his name, and that made him square with the Texas Department of Corrections. Beyond that, his name was on a need-to-know basis, and as far as Bobby Peveto was concerned, no one else needed to know.

So to the rest of the world, Bobby Peveto was simply Bo.

'Cept for Dorothy Jo, of course. Dorothy Jo Devereaux was the mom he'd always wished for. His own had died when he was in the second grade, and even those young memories of her were faded. He'd prefer his last name was Devereaux, anyway.

In Bobby's opinion, Lawrence Devereaux, Dorothy Jo's real son, had been a stupid son of a bitch.

Bo took his job at the Fire and Ice House seriously, because that job kept him out of Huntsville where he'd first met Dorothy Jo. She'd come in to visit her son one day. Lawrence had been in solitary for something or other, so she'd asked to visit someone who never got visitors. Bo had hated her at first, liked her after a fashion, loved her more than anything when she'd gone before the Parole Board and said she was a cook at an ice house whose owner had agreed to hire Bobby Peveto if they'd let him out. They balked when they heard it was a bartending job, but they weren't stupid, either. Besides, the judge was one of Angie's regulars, and he signed the papers. Bo couldn't drink what he sold, but for seven years he'd made a living wage, which was more than most ex-cons could say.

Maybe it was Bo's experience that had his antennae going up when the man in the gray slacks and blue windbreaker walked tentatively into the noisy Saturday night bar mob. He looked uncomfortable as hell, Bo noted. The stranger's face was tinged pink as if he was standing too close to a fire, but it was his hands, fidgeting at his lapel and exposing the hint of a clerical collar, that told Bo this man was in the wrong place.

"You need somethin'?" Bo pushed away from the bar.

The man's gaze darted around the crowded room, then at the floor, then up to Bo. "I was looking for . . . Miss . . . Unh . . . Angie."

Bo's eyes narrowed. "You got business with her?"

"Business?" The pastor's voice actually cracked. "No," he stammered. "No business."

"Then what do you want her for?" Bo planted both feet firmly on the ground.

"I think I found her dog," the man blurted out.

Bo relaxed. The stranger might be bringing news about Maeve O'Day. Angie was worried sick about her missing mother. "Angie's in the kitchen."

"I . . . the kitchen?"

"Through there." Bo jabbed his thumb at the swinging doors behind the bar, then went to the customer holding up his glass for another draft.

Matt Hayden blew out a sigh of relief and walked through the swinging doors into the kitchen of the O'Day Fire and Ice House. The first thing that struck him was the utter white of the room. The linoleum, the walls, the appliances, the shelves were all white. The second thing that struck him was the smell of bleach and disinfectant. The small clinic Wilks called a hospital didn't smell this clean.

"Miss O'Day?" he said into the seemingly empty room.

There was a rustle of noise from behind a door, then a number of loud bumps.

Matt gulped. Surely she wasn't conducting business in a broom closet, he thought.

What emerged from behind the door, however, was a significantly clothed, rag-holding, bucket-carrying Angie O'Day. Her jeans and T-shirt were dirty white; she wore green rubber gloves on her hands.

She took one look at him and scowled.

Angie O'Day didn't want to be bothered with a lunatic clergyman on a mission from God. Her mother was missing, and her kitchen was under the constant scrutiny of the local authorities. It didn't matter that it was a Saturday night and half the town was in her bar to party. Angie O'Day wasn't in a good mood.

"Kitchen's off-limits to customers," she said sharply. She grabbed her bucket and walked to the sink.

"Miss O'Day . . ." Matt Hayden wasn't sure where to begin his bad news. Contrary to popular belief, the seminary did not always train a minister as to what should be said when—especially when—foul play might be involved.

"State your business, then get out."

The pastor nodded. "I think I've found your dog."

Angie came instantly alert. "Shadow?"

"I'm sorry, Miss O'Day." Angie saw the troubled look in his eyes and knew a deeper level of fear than she'd experienced all day.

Matt's voice was quiet against the noise of the Saturday night crowd. "He's in the church parking lot. I think you'd better come with me."

"Is he hurt?" Angie was already pulling off her rubber gloves and heading for the door.

"That's just it, Miss O'Day. He has blood all over him," Matt said as he looked her straight in the eye, "but I can't find a scratch on him."

***

Sheriff Novak's blue eyes hinted at the German blood of his mother's family, while the glint in them came wholly from his father's Czech side. That was how James W. spent most of his life—torn between the sober side of him that was Wilks and the fun-loving side that was Novak.

None of the Novak was showing now, however, as he crouched over the bloodied dog. Angie O'Day stood over his left shoulder, holding her elbows, her face pale. Pastor Hayden held a dripping garden hose behind them. "Helluva lotta blood, all right," James W. agreed. He brushed his hand through the dog's wet fur. "No wound."

"That's why I called you." Matt Hayden nodded. "Something . . . or somebody . . . out there has lost a lot of blood."

James W. cleared his throat awkwardly.

"You mean . . . Mamma?" Angie asked, trying to control the shiver in her voice. The two men stared in silence at the animal as it lapped at the Tupperware bowl of water Matt had filled.

"I looked around for another animal—thought maybe this one had gotten in a fight . . ." Matt let the words hang.

Shadow laid his head down on the grass, his sides heaving as he fought for breath.

"Shadow might not be wounded," the sheriff said, "but he's plenty sick. He needs to be taken to a vet."

"Is there a veterinarian in town?" Matt asked.

"Nope," Angie answered for the sheriff. "Closest one is in Bastrop."

"I can take him," Matt offered.

"I don't need your help," Angie snapped angrily, then turned on the sheriff. Her voice softened appreciably. "What about Mamma?"

"This puts her disappearin' into a whole new light," James W. thought aloud. "It's after six o'clock," he continued, looking at his watch. "Dang, it's gonna be hard doin' this in the dark."

"I can maybe get you some reinforcements at church tomorrow, if the search is still on," said Matt.

"That might be my mother's blood, and you're gonna let her stay out in the cold all night?" Angie demanded.

"She's probably holed up in somebody's house." James W. put his arm around her shoulder for reassurance. "You know how many people go into Houston or Austin for the weekends." He let out a chuckle. "Heck, I'll go over and see if Ernie knows anything."

"Ernie Masterson?" Matt asked in surprise.

Trying to lighten the tone, the sheriff smiled. "Ernie'll be able to tell me who's out of town. He knows everything about everybody. Found a gamblin' receipt in Joe Crowder's car one time. Figured out Crowder wasn't workin' in Angus, but playin' craps in Lake Charles. Pumped gas for Sarah Fullenweider—your secretary's daughter. He saw a suitcase in the back seat and knew a divorce was in the works. He puts two and two together. It's uncanny."

"He's a horrible man," Angie said with disgust. "I wouldn't put it past him to drive Mamma out of town as some kind of joke."

"Ernie's harmless," James W. said, patting her on the

shoulder. "And your mamma is probably fine. Even if she is lost, don't forget what a fighter she is."

"Then how do you explain what's happened to Shadow?" Angie felt a fresh spurt of tears behind her eyes, but she fought them back. She knelt down and patted her dog. Shadow looked at her as if pleading with her to do something.

"I'll lay you odds Shadow got himself a raccoon," James W. said. "Preacher, those reinforcements might be a good idea. Why don't you announce that we'll get together at the Muster Tree after services."

"The Muster Tree?"

"The big oak in the middle of the square," Angie explained. "It's where everybody gathers to go to war or to put together search parties."

"You mean you've had to do this kind of thing before?" Matt asked.

"Did it thirty-five years ago when my pa went missing," James W. said.

Matt looked up sharply. "Where'd you find him?"

James W. slapped his hat on his head. "Never did."

***

"What if she's dead, Dorothy Jo?" Angie O'Day posed the question into the two a.m. silence of the closed Fire and Ice House. Bleach and pine-scented cleaner suffused the darkness. The only light in the room came from the Christmas lights overhead and the blue and red neon of the Pabst Blue Ribbon sign on the bar's back mirror.

Also visible in that mirror were the tired images of Angie O'Day and Dorothy Jo Devereaux. Instead of the usual iced tea they drank at the end of a long night and wash down, both women sat at the bar, a shot glass of whiskey before each, and a bottle of Jim Beam between them.

"Let's not borrow trouble, Angie," Dorothy Jo said. She tapped the pack of generic cigarettes on the bar, then pulled one out with her lips. "She's a strong woman, Maeve O'Day."

"Was." Angie shook her head. "She's turned fragile these last few months. More confused. Heck, if she's havin' one of her spells, she won't even be able to tell anyone her name, much less where she lives."

"James W. is out there right now." Dorothy Jo lit her cigarette with a flick of her lighter. "He's got both his deputies with him. They'll find her."

Angie studied the weathered old woman who sat beside her. Dorothy Jo was the most important person in her life next to her mamma. The stocky cook had come to work the day the doors to the Fire and Ice House opened, and missed few since. She'd taken one day off to see her daughter get married over in Pflugerville ten years back. Another one to put her husband in the ground about the same time Angie took over the reins at the Fire and Ice House. Finally, she'd gone up to Huntsville the day her son had been executed for first degree murder.

Dorothy Jo Devereaux was as much a part of the Fire and Ice House as Angie was, and Angie had lived her whole life in the small apartment above the bar. Maeve had bought the firehouse from the town in a closed bidding before anyone in

Wilks knew she was even interested in the place. All hell broke out when Maeve opened a bar right across the river from Miss Olivia's precious Lutheran Church. The brouhaha was one of the highlights of Maeve's life.

And the last time Wilks held a closed bidding on any business matter.

The memories of the story brought a smile to Angie's face, and her thoughts turned hopeful. "If Shadow gets better, he can sniff her out. He's a good dog."

"He's a great dog," Dorothy Jo reassured her.

Angie smiled. "Thanks again for comin' in tonight while Bo took him to Bastrop."

"I'd have whupped you if you hadn't let me know."

Angie took the first sip of her drink and felt it burn down her throat. The sensation matched the stinging in eyes that were too raw to cry anymore.

Not that she'd let anyone see her cry.

Besides, it was probably the bleach. She just had the cleanest kitchen in Wilks, Texas, that was all.

"I guess that preacher thinks I'm the worst kind of scum, sendin' my mamma out with my dog for a walk."

"Honey, you been doin' that for four years. Your mamma loves those walks. Nobody in Wilks would let her come to harm."

"Til today."

"We don't know that."

"Lord, Dorothy Jo, what if that was my mamma's blood all over Shadow?" The sob escaped from Angie before she could hold it back. She rested her forehead in her hand. "My mamma's my only kin, Dorothy Jo. I haven't got anybody else."

"I know, honey."

"She's always been there for me. Lord," Angie said as she raised her head, "what am I gonna do without her?"

Angie looked into the mirror, her gaze scanning the reflected restaurant. "She bought this place, fixed it up, kept it goin' so I could have somethin'. So I wouldn't be left with nothin' like she was."

Angie slumped. "I don't want it, Dorothy Jo. Not without Mamma. I want my mamma."

Dorothy Jo put her withered hand on Angie's back and rubbed. With her other hand, she puffed on her cigarette. Dorothy Jo shook her head as Angie's sobs filled the room. She didn't know how to deal with her own feelings about the missing Maeve O'Day, much less Angie's.

"What do you think that preacher man was doin' in here today?" Dorothy Jo asked finally.

Angie's head came up with a snap. "I don't care. Anytime that man wants to pass my place, I'll appreciate it."

Dorothy Jo smiled inwardly. The best way to get Angie O'Day out of a funk was to spark her Irish temper. "He's gonna help recruit people for the search party tomorrow," Dorothy Jo egged on.

"Tomorrow's gonna be a day late and a dollar short. If he really cared, he'd be callin' people tonight to get them to help."

"Now, honey, even James W. said that it'd be easier to search for her in the daytime."

"I don't give a damn about easy. It's supposed to get down to fifty degrees tonight, and my mother's out in the cold, maybe wounded. They need to be looking for her right now." Angie pounded her fist on the bar.

The front door to the Fire and Ice House squeaked open. Bobby Peveto walked in, his dark blue bandanna tied around his forehead Indian-style, his face hard as stone. "I left Shadow at the vet's. He's gonna make it."

"What's wrong with him?" Angie asked.

"The vet agreed there wasn't a scratch on him." Bo came around the bar, filled a glass with ice and squirted himself a Coca Cola from the bar hose.

"Why was he so sick, then?" Angie pressed.

"The vet says we might even be able to get him back in the mornin'. Vet's got Shadow on an IV, cleanin' out his system." Bo took a long drink of his soda.

Angie sat straighter in her chair. It was the first time she'd ever seen Bo evade a direct question.

Seven years ago, when she'd interviewed him at the state pen for his job, she'd been new and he'd been less gray. But both of them had seen enough of life not to waste time on pleasantries. Already knowing about the manslaughter conviction, she'd straight-out asked him for what crime he'd done time.

"I killed a man, Miss O'Day," he'd said. His back had been straight. His eyes clear.

"What for?" she'd asked.

"Raping my sister. Only blood I had."

Angie had understood that answer. In Bobby Peveto she'd

found a soul mate. If anyone ever laid a hand on her mother, Angie O'Day would do the same thing.

Kill.

She had hired Bobby Peveto, murderer and Texas Department of Corrections parolee, on the spot, pending the judge's release.

That same man who'd admitted to murder without pause wasn't answering Angie's question.

"Bo, what is wrong with my dog?" Angie demanded, her voice hard, hiding the growing fear in her heart.

He put down the glass. "The vet said whoever did it hadn't given Shadow enough to kill him." Bo looked Angie straight in the eye. "There's no doubt it was intentional. It was wrapped up in a ball of raw hamburger."

"What are you talkin' about?"

"Wasp poison."

Chapter Four
Love and the Muster Tree

Elsbeth Novak, wife of James W., stood at Matt's church office the next morning before the ten-thirty worship. Her well-rounded form was tightly cinched into a double-breasted brown suede suit, and the double strand of large pearls at her neck made sure the world knew she had money.

She looked the picture of gluttony, Matt thought as he sorted through the keys for the one that fit his office door. Smelled it, too, he realized with disgust. She had enough perfume on to perform duty in a funeral parlor.

"I need a minute of your time." Elsbeth followed him into his office.

"A minute's about all I have," Matt said, glancing at his watch. He'd gotten a late start on his sermon last night, after finding Shadow in the church parking lot and going back to Angie's. Of course, he'd already written one for today, but last night's events had provided new inspiration. The fact that he'd skipped breakfast to make it to church on time added to his discomfort.

"I'm here about next Sunday. Lay Sunday?" Elsbeth settled herself with a squeak into the black upholstered chair opposite Matt's desk. "I have the best news!"

He looked impatiently out the door as the sound of voices increased in the narthex. He should be getting his robes on for the service.

"Jimmy Jr. is comin' to town next Sunday!" Elsbeth said triumphantly.

That caught Matt's attention. He laid the sermon folder on his desk. "The soon-to-be- governor, Jimmy Jr.?" He smiled. "I look forward to meeting him."

"You're not just goin' to meet him," Elsbeth said with excitement. "He's decided to preach!"

"Preach?" Matt echoed, the wind sucked out of him.

"It's Lay Sunday, Reverend! Isn't that perfect?"

"We already have three lay people lined up with talks, five minutes each."

"Oh, five minutes would never do," Elsbeth continued. "Jimmy Jr. has a whole platform he can talk about. His campaign theme is 'Do unto others.' That's right out of the Bible!"

"Yes, I know, Mrs. Novak." Matt felt his neck start to redden.

"The media is travelin' with him now. You should see all the attention he's gettin'. *Texas Monthly* is even doin' a story about the family!" Elsbeth went on. "Think of what that'll do for evangelism for Grace."

Matt listened to her chatter, all the while counting in his

mind the length of the next week's service. Besides the three lay people who were giving talks, two choirs would be singing, and Warren Yeck, bless him, was doing the prayers. Warren, who served as part-time custodian for Grace Lutheran, was a mastermind with a hammer and nail, but it took him twenty words to say what most folks could cover in three.

Now Elsbeth wanted her son to use the service as a campaign stop.

"Perhaps you could give me your son's phone number," Matt said, thinking that a dinner after Sunday service might be a better forum for the gubernatorial candidate.

"He can't be bothered with phone calls, Preacher. I'll make all of the arrangements. It'll be wonderful. You'll see." She grabbed her expensive leather handbag and stood. "By the way, my husband said somethin' about your being over at the Fire and Ice House last night. Even after I talked to you about That Woman yesterday afternoon. I've decided, however, I don't need to mention that to Miss Olivia. You know how she feels about that place."

She headed for the door, then turned back, a victorious smile on her face. "I'll tell Jimmy Jr. that you're delighted about next Sunday. Thanks for your time, Reverend."

***

One of the things Matt enjoyed most about being a preacher was Sunday morning worship. To be sure, many clergy dreaded the exercise. Choirs and Bible readings and sermons needed coordination. Ushers and acolytes had to be recruited and trained. And every parishioner seemed to have some tidbit of business that they'd saved up for Sunday when they saw the preacher.

For Matt, however, the Sunday morning experience was exciting and worshipful. Sure it was hectic, he acknowledged, but for the most part it was people coming together to celebrate God. Everyone had an opinion on how this or that should be done, of course, but the very fact that they had an opinion meant they cared.

This Sunday was the celebration of Epiphany. Matt would talk, sing, pray and meditate about the very thing that fascinated him most about God.

Love.

After Warren Yeck finished with the gospel reading, Matt got up from his seat in the front pew. He climbed the four stairs to the stage that held the pulpit on the right, the lectern to the left and, straight ahead, the altar which was elevated another three steps. Above the altar was an intricate stained glass window depicting Christ as the Good Shepherd.

He walked to the pulpit which was carved in the same dark oak as the altar. Matt had preached fourteen sermons from this pulpit since he'd arrived at Grace. Six Sunday mornings' worth, four midweek Advent, two services Christmas Eve, one Christmas morning and one New Year's Eve. Every one of those sermons had followed the gospel for the day to the letter. Every one of them would have made his seminary instructors proud. They'd been theologically truthful. Scripturally sound.

And, very possibly, blatantly boring.

His congregation seemed pleased with Matt ever since he'd arrived. He'd like to think it was because he was a good minister. He suspected it was because he hadn't asked them to think much about their own ministry.

The honeymoon was about to end.

As the last strains of the sermon hymn echoed from the congregation, Matt bowed his head in silent prayer.

The congregation waited expectantly for the safe, old story of the Wise Men visiting the baby Jesus—the event that marked Epiphany. Folks sat comfortably in their pews, legs crossed, eyes raised in contented curiosity; a few blew their noses in anticipation of the silence that should accompany the sermon of the day.

Matt looked off to his left. The Yeck brothers, Warren and Ben, sat in the very last pew, ready to fix a squeaky microphone or adjust a dimmer on a light switch as needed. Pearl and Ernie Masterson were in their appointed pew—lectern side, fourth row back from the pillar that marked the halfway point of the sanctuary. Sundays were the only days Matt saw Ernie Masterson out from under the slime of his garage, though Matt still felt a touch of grease always remained somewhere on Ernie's countenance. Other Sunday morning regulars sat in their customary spots, ritual rather than choice dictating their seating arrangement.

Finally, Matt let his gaze fall on the second pew from the front, pulpit side. Though three members of the Wilks clan usually took up the seats nearest the center aisle, today only Elsbeth Novak and Miss Olivia sat in the pew.

James W. was still out looking for Maeve O'Day.

Matt drew a deep breath. "Epiphany," he said, looking out over the congregation. He let the word hang in the air while over a hundred and fifty pairs of eyes stared back at him. "The time we celebrate the Three Wise Men following the Star, fulfilling their destiny, and finding the baby Jesus.

"What is our destiny? What is it about Epiphany that we can celebrate in our own lives today?"

He scanned the faces of his congregation. After six weeks, he knew most of his parishioners by name.

"It's very simple, dear brothers and sisters in Christ. Jesus told us to love God with all of our hearts, minds and souls. And then he said to love each other as we love ourselves. When we do as Jesus commanded, we fulfill our own destiny."

He looked at the second row. Miss Olivia, her sharp eyes and sharper chin pointed directly at him. Next to her, Elsbeth Novak furrowed her brow in curiosity.

He held her gaze for a solemn moment before continuing.

"Today we have a special opportunity to show that love to a fellow member of our community. As many of you have heard, Maeve O'Day, a victim of Alzheimer's disease and a longtime resident of Wilks, Texas, is missing."

His voice softened. "I understand you've all met at the Muster Tree before—another time, another missing person."

He allowed his gaze to connect with Elsbeth Novak's. There was no doubt as to her level of emotion. Whereas Miss Olivia's face was white as her hair, Elsbeth's was as red as the hymnal she held in her lap. "Bad times bring a community together," he said more in one last plea to the two women rather than to the total of the gathering before him.

"As a congregation, we can show the love of Christ to this community. Though this may not be the first time we've had to look for a lost member of Wilks, we can all pray this is the last."

Chapter Five
On the Scent

"Cold day," Matt called out as he stepped over the sidewalk chain.

James W. looked up from the map he studied under the tall live oak that dominated Wilks Town Square and snorted. He'd gotten an earful from his wife about the new pastor's sermon. James W. was loath to risk Elsbeth's anger by having a jovial conversation with the preacher in eyesight of his mother's house, where he knew Elsbeth and Miss Olivia were watching the activities on the Square. He shrugged off the notion, however. He was the sheriff. His wife was . . . sometimes . . . a pain in the neck.

James W. stuck his hands in the front pockets of his wrinkled khaki uniform pants and nodded. "Gonna be colder," he said. "Norther's blowin' through. We'll be lucky if Shadow gets a scent before it rains."

"Shadow's all right, then?" Matt asked.

"Weaker than hell," James W. said and pushed off the

bumper of his four-door truck. "Let's get this shindig started," he called to the group of fifty that had gathered around the tree.

He waited wearily while his deputies passed around maps and coordinated cell phone numbers. He'd been up all night looking for Maeve O'Day. He had a bad feeling about not being able to find the old woman.

It reminded him too much of the futile search conducted thirty-five years earlier for his father.

That search party had started out small as well, no one really thinking any harm had come to Cash Novak. Danny Don Dube had been the sheriff. James W., just twenty-five years of age, was the newest deputy on Danny Don's staff. After a full day and night of searching, however, Danny Don had called together a search party. Like today, a good number of townsfolk had come out. More on horses back then.

On that day as well, the weather had also been cold and getting colder—a late-spring cold spell in April 1980.

The month from which his family had never recovered.

April 1980 was the month the entire nation had plummeted into despair at word that President Carter's attempt to free the American hostages in Iran had failed with the death of eight soldiers. Then the next day, a Saturday James W. would never forget, word that his brother was one of those killed in the rescue attempt had been delivered by a uniformed colonel from Fort Hood and Pastor Osterburg, then the pastor of Grace Lutheran. Roth Novak, James W.'s older brother, was dead.

Suddenly the grief of a nation held hostage became personal. No longer was the pain he felt only for the Americans "over there." Now his anguish was for the American that would never return. His half-brother.

Miss Olivia had been alone that day when the news came. Cash Novak was a mover and a shaker in Texas politics although he'd never held office and had still been in Houston after the Reagan/Carter Presidential debate. There were no cell phones back then. Ernie Masterson had finally found a friend of a friend who knew where Cash was. Ernie gave Cash the news of Roth's death and supposedly Cash had left Houston immediately to come back to Wilks. He never made it home.

One stunning event after another. In a way, James W. had never recovered from those events. In one swoop, he'd become an only child and a son with no pa. As much as it affected him, however, James W. knew that his mother changed in her very soul. He'd known Miss Olivia to be stern before April of 1980. Thinking back now, however, he struggled to remember a time since then that Miss Olivia had laughed.

None came to mind.

"Split into parties of twos and threes." James W. pulled himself from his memories when he realized the crowd was staring at him expectantly. "Warren, you take the church van and load up the first aid equipment. Every group should have my cell number on speed dial, and don't be textin' to anybody else while we're looking. Y'all got your assignments on the maps Richard gave you. Questions?"

James W. surveyed the crowd. A good portion of them looked to be members from Grace Lutheran. "Thanks for the help, Preacher," he said in an aside to Matt, then turned back to the crowd. "Let's go!"

***

"I heard what you did in church today," Angie said as she gave her dog a drink from the jug she carried. For two miles she'd walked wordlessly between the pastor and the sheriff as Shadow led the group west, passed the Yeck Feed Store, the broken-down trailer park where Dorothy Jo Devereaux lived and on out toward open country. The group had come to a rest stop at a clump of trees, when they realized Shadow was leading them up the entrance ramp to Interstate 71.

Matt shrugged. "It seemed like the Christian thing to do."

"Some people in that church don't give a hoot about what's the Christian thing to do." She put the cap back on the jug and patted Shadow's head. He had Mamma's scent all right. The dog had set a fast pace for the group to follow.

"Your dog knows right where he's going," Matt said, as if reading her mind.

"He's a good huntin' dog," Angie allowed.

"Good hunting dogs are hard to come by."

"Not as hard as good people." She turned on her heel and walked away. She couldn't figure the preacher out, and right now she didn't want to try. All she could think about was her mamma. How far out in the country Shadow had already led them. How her frail mother could never have walked this far out of town.

"Is Shadow all right?" James W. joined them.

"He's angry we stopped," Angie said.

Indeed, it looked as if Shadow was impatient to get going again. The dog stood on the ramp, pulling against his leash first to the right of the road, then the left.

"He's gonna wear himself out," James W. said. "The vet said he's nowhere near bein' well."

"We could ride until the first exit," Matt suggested.

"He'll lose the scent," Angie said in disgust.

"He'll pick it up again if it's there," Matt answered. "If it's not, we'll know we've gone too far."

James W. crooked his head. "You know about bloodhounds, Preacher?"

"I know about search dogs. My brother was a cop in . . . Denver. Kept a dog to sniff out drugs and . . ." He looked at Angie and stopped. "Whatever."

"Dead bodies," Angie finished for him.

Matt bowed his head. "Sometimes."

James W. turned to the search party. "Saddle up or get in a truck. We're headin' out."

The group headed up the entrance ramp. Matt watched from his perch in the back seat of the sheriff's truck as the odometer tripped one mile, then two before coming to the first exit for Schulenburg.

"This is stupid." Angie sat in the front of the cab. "Mamma couldn't have walked this far. She sure as hell didn't have to wait for an exit to get off the highway. On foot she could've taken off anywhere."

"She wasn't on foot," Matt said quietly.

"What?" The sheriff's head snapped around.

"Shadow's been getting the scent from the bushes and grass. He's crossing from one side of the road to the other trying to get a better trail. Your mamma's scent came out of a car's air filtration system."

"But that means someone drove . . ." Angie let the words hang.

"Yeah. It does."

***

James W. pulled his truck over to the side of the Interstate. "I hope this works, Pastor," he said as Angie jumped from the cab to get her dog out of the truck's long bed. "Those clouds look like they're gonna drop rain any minute."

The search party had traveled a full eight miles out of Wilks. Three times on its trek down Interstate 71, they stopped at exit ramps to see if Shadow could detect Maeve O'Day's scent. At the last stop, the dog had gone in circles, sniffed the air, the truck, Angie.

Shadow had lost the scent. James W. had told the search party to turn around and head back to the previous exit.

Now the group stood at the Highway 159 exit ramp.

Despite his resting in the truck's bed between exits, Shadow looked like he was failing fast. His brown-and-black coat clung to his heaving sides. His tongue hung low to the ground, and his nostrils flared widely in rhythm with his panting.

"Richard, follow us in the truck," James W. barked to the deputy who'd been tending Shadow in the back.

Matt jumped down from the Dodge and stretched. As he looked to the sky, he saw ominous clouds approaching from the north, three times darker and more intense than the already heavy clouds that hung overhead.

A nasty storm was on its way.

He had little time to muse on the weather, however, as Angie, James W. and Shadow headed down the ramp. Matt jogged to catch up with them, then walked wordlessly beside them as Shadow strained at the leash.

"He's on the scent now," James W. observed.

Shadow led them a half mile down the asphalt, then turned north onto a dirt road marked "Heller Road." Finally, after a mile, the group came to a halt at a line of barbed-wire fence with the posted sign "No Trespassing."

James W. put hands to hips and blew out a frustrated breath.

"You're the sheriff. You can ignore a no trespassin' sign," Angie said.

James W. bowed his head and looked at the ground. "Not when it's a deer lease, Angie," he said quietly.

"Deer lease?" Matt echoed.

"Farmers lease their land to hunters for deer season," James W. explained. "There's thousands of acres around here that haven't been cleared for pasture."

"I thought deer season was in November."

"Starts in November." James W. looked helplessly at Angie. "Ends at sundown today."

"That rain's not gonna hold until sundown," she said quietly. "James W., please, Shadow will lose the scent."

"Can we find out who owns this property?" Matt interjected. "Maybe no one's hunting on it this weekend."

James W. dropped his gaze. "I already know who owns this

property. This used to be Novak land. Not Wilks." He chuckled humorlessly. "My mother always said it like that."

"Used to be? Who owns it now?" Matt pressed.

"After my father died . . ." James W. cleared his throat uncomfortably. "My mother sold it to Ernie Masterson."

Chapter Six
Not My Problem

"Ernie, it's for you." Pearl Masterson brought the phone to her husband where he sat in his lounger. She hated to bother him. Sundays were sacred to Ernie. She could barely keep him at church long enough for the final hymn before he was heading across the street to their apartment to catch the TV's pre-game football analysis.

"Dammit, Pearl . . ." Ernie swiped the phone from her hand. "What?" he barked into the receiver.

Pearl tiptoed back into the kitchen, despite the fact the television blared loudly from the front room. She noticed that Ernie finally turned the volume down when he heard who was calling.

"Yeah, Richard, what's so all-fired-up important?" Ernie asked the deputy.

Pearl went to the refrigerator and pulled out another beer, then grabbed a frosted mug from the freezer. Ernie's glass was almost empty.

"Yeah, I got it rented. To a damned Yankee." Disgust mixed with disdain resonated in Ernie's chuckle. Even Pearl had to admit the man from Michigan had sounded like he didn't know much about hunting.

"I'm supposed to pick him up at 4:00. Later if the game's not over. Why?"

Hating to break a nail, Pearl used a can opener to pop open the beer, then poured it into the mug. She scrunched her nose at the sour smell. Thank goodness, Ernie hadn't made her drink one for a while.

"He'll shoot at anything that moves," Ernie said. "The man's an idiot."

Pearl brought the beer to Ernie as he hung up the phone.

"Gotta go to the deer lease," Ernie said. He looked at the drink she held. "What's that for?"

"Your beer was gettin' low."

Ernie shook his head. "I gotta go. Don't waste that one, baby. Drink it down."

Pearl looked at the drink, repulsed.

"That's right," Ernie said. "Beer ain't your style. You like convicts better. Beer-pourin', murderin' convicts."

"Ernie, I was just talking to Bo after he brought you home the other night. That's all."

"After he punched me."

Pearl held her tongue. She knew Bo had been forced to manhandle Ernie to get him out of a brawl over at the Fire and Ice House Thursday night. Bo had probably saved him from a far worse beating at the hands of Zach Gibbons, the meanest man in Wilks.

Ernie opened the front door. "Go ahead and drink that beer, Pearl baby. Maybe when I come home you'll feel as friendly toward me as you do to that ex-con."

Pearl suppressed a shiver. Most likely there was nothing to be afraid of. On the way back from the lease, Ernie would probably have a few at the Ice House and come home ready to pass out. "Are there problems at the deer lease?" she asked instead.

Ernie smiled. It was a cold smile. "Not mine."

Chapter Seven
Taking a Punch

James W. walked through the search party as they awaited Ernie Masterson's arrival. Matt watched the sheriff give instructions and pats on the back as he went. James W. offered an encouraging word to Warren Yeck, who had the hood of the church van up and was pounding with pliers on the engine. For the first time since Matt had known him, James W. looked worried.

"It's all right." Angie O'Day comforted her dog as she brought the water bottle to his mouth. Shadow looked at her, then turned impatiently back toward the fence.

"He's a keeper," Matt said.

"I don't need you tellin' me that. He's my dog."

Matt watched the young woman bite back her tears and knew that anger was the only thing that kept her in control of her emotions.

He'd always been a curious fellow. At least that's what his mother, Jewel Hogan, used to say. Now his curiosity might be satisfied at the same time he gave Angie the only kind of help from him she would accept.

"I was wondering, Miss O'Day," Matt said. "Do you dislike pastors in general, or is there something about me in particular that bothers you?"

Angie's gaze flared with anger, and Matt knew he had accomplished his goal. Angie O'Day had a good Irish temper.

"Both," she snapped.

"Care to talk about it?"

"Like you give a damn?"

Matt leaned against the bumper of James W.'s truck. "I'm curious."

"I know exactly what you holier-than-thous have under that pious appearance you put on to the world. Nothin'. No heart. No soul. Just a bunch of hypocrisy." Angie screwed the lid on the water bottle and spit.

"You don't know me well enough to know if I'm a hypocrite or not."

"I know your kind." She slung her backpack over her shoulder. "Known you ever since I was five years old." She stalked off toward the barbed-wire fence. Shadow followed closely at her heels.

Matt decided pursuit was his only choice if he wanted to find the underlying cause of what was bugging Angie O'Day. He pushed off the truck bumper.

The wind kicked up clouds of dust and sent them scurrying across the dirt road. With the wind came the wild scent of earth and crops and animals. Matt breathed in and felt its untamed violence stir something deep inside of him. His gaze stayed on Angie and he realized in that moment that Angie was at one with this place. She was as wild and natural as the wind that howled around her, blowing the flames of her hair toward the thunderous sky overhead. He swallowed hard. If he wasn't careful, he might be falling into dangerous territory in his feelings about this woman.

Angie walked through the dust, impervious to its grit. She came to a halt at the barbed-wire fence and hitched her boot on its bottom line. Matt realized he was looking at one of the strongest women he had ever met.

The thought had him taking a good swallow before challenging her again. "What happened when you were five years old?" he asked, coming up beside her.

"None of your damned business."

"If it's what you're holding against me, it is."

Angie turned on him. She looked angry and wild and brave. Her red hair flared in the wind like a bright flame. Her eyes were brown and steady. She had no fear in her, he realized.

"I was a guest at your church once. Grace. Great name for a church." She laughed humorlessly.

"When you were five years old?"

She nodded. "The guest of Delia Yeck. Warren's granddaughter." Angie stared out onto the grass field beyond the fence. "She and I were classmates at kindergarten."

"Go on."

"Her Sunday school teacher was Miss Olivia Wilks-Novak." Angie's voice grew terse. "The great lady of Wilks—owns Grace

and the whole damned town. Except for Mamma's Ice House."
Angie looked back to the field. "At the Sunday school openin',
we sang this song about how Jesus loves the little children. All
the children of the world. Red and yellow, black, and
white . . ."

"I know the song."

"Then Miss Olivia went to the front of the church and called
me up to join her. I was real honored. Here I was a guest, and
I was goin' to be introduced to everybody."

Matt swallowed uncomfortably.

"Miss Olivia, she turned me around to face the whole Sunday
school. She proceeded to tell them all that I was the daughter of a
prostitute." Angie glared hard at Matt. "She grabbed me by the
hand, jerked me all the way down that aisle and out the front door
of the church. Said God didn't want sinful little children like me
in his church."

Matt bowed his head.

"The whole time, the kids laughed at me. They laughed at
me the next day at school. And for years after that. And they
threw dirt on me, first the real stuff off the ground, then later
the kind that comes out of people's mouths. They said I was
dirty."

Angie's pain, still fresh and deep even thirty years later, was
almost tangible to Matt. For the first time since he'd met her,
Matt realized Angie was as vulnerable as she was strong.

"I'm sorry," he said, finally.

"You don't have anything to be sorry for," Angie said,
impatiently wiping at a tear that threatened to drop. "I didn't

believe her. My mamma told me not to believe her. Mamma told me that I was beautiful. That I'd been made in love." This time a tear did slip down her cheek. "She told me that God loved me very much."

Matt mustered a smile. "Your mamma must be a very special person."

Angie stared hard at him, and all vulnerability drained from her face. With a determined move, she raised her hand, then swung it with all of her might against his cheek. "I don't need you, or your approval of my mother."

Matt's gaze locked with hers. His face stung from the strong slap.

Slowly, to make sure she understood his gesture, he turned his other cheek toward her and closed his eyes.

He held the pose for a full second, then another. Waiting for the next slap.

He realized only too late that Angie O'Day wasn't one to be told what to do. Even in the offer of the other cheek.

Instead, he felt her balled fist hit his gut only a moment before the second blow caught him full in the solar plexus. The air rushed from his body. With the helplessness of a jelly fish, he fell to the ground. So stunned was he by her punches that he hit the dirt with his mouth open. He got a full taste of Texas clay for his troubles. Amid a chorus of distant snickers from the onlookers, Matt rolled onto his back, counting his bones to make sure none were broken. "Feel better?" he asked, spitting out the grit that coated his teeth and tongue.

"Some."

He lay back against the ground and realized he'd barely missed falling on the barbed-wire fence. God was looking out for him after all, he realized. Matt had kind of wondered where the Almighty had been a moment earlier.

Then his gaze caught on the middle wire of the fence, and all thought of pain left him. "Get the sheriff." He rolled to his knees and crawled closer to inspect the fence. Fear filled him as he gingerly touched a finger to the rusted metal. He pulled his hand away to study it.

"What is it?" Angie asked, alarmed.

Matt looked from his hand to her face.

"Blood."

Chapter Eight
Damn Yankee

Chip Carouthers was a man of purpose, good-looking at six foot two with still-blonde hair. Above all, he was intelligent. At least that was what he told himself every day of his CFO job at the tire factory up in Detroit, Michigan. He surrounded himself with the most talented people he could find, though every one of them knew less and less the more he got to know them. His wife, who had once been pretty and smart, had only gotten uglier and dumber as their marriage of twelve years had endured.

Because he was totally surrounded by nincompoops every day of his life, he'd decided that for once he was going to have a vacation where he could spend time with his one and only favorite person.

Chip Carouthers.

To that end, he'd had the company librarian do an Internet search of Texas hunting leases. When his wife and kids became unbearable last Christmas Eve, he'd decided to give himself a special Christmas present. He deserved to get out from behind the desk and back to basics on a vacation. What could be more basic than a hunting trip?

Man versus animal. Brain versus brawn. A weapon that gave purchase when balanced in a warrior's arm, held against the shoulder. A campfire at night to cook the day's prey. Living off the product of the hunt, sleeping under a starlit sky. That was what Chip needed. He knew it instinctively.

At least it must be instinctive, he figured, since he'd never before been hunting.

Sure enough, after weeks of waiting for that lazy librarian's research, Chip had a list of deer leases available in the Texas Hill Country. He'd called down the list, and finally hit on the perfect vacation spot. Four hundred acres of land all to himself for three whole days. The price had been a little heftier than some of the other plots for lease, but that only insured him a good location, right?

Somewhere, however, something had gone terribly wrong.

Chip Carouthers stared at the dying embers of the fire before him. He was in his sleeping bag, buck naked. His clothes hung across the bushes that surrounded the small clearing he'd called home for the last three days. He prayed they would be dry before that idiot hick who had leased him this god-forsaken acreage came to pick him up. He held in his hand a cup of tea. He wanted coffee, but couldn't stomach the stuff he'd tried to cook up that morning. Who the hell knew how to make coffee without electricity?

It had all been that stupid dog's fault. Chip had spent all day

Friday getting the feel of his weapon. He'd never held a rifle before. Or was this a shotgun? That sales clerk in Houston had made a big deal that rifles and shotguns weren't the same thing, but Chip finally blew him off. The gun was long and had a trigger. It could kill.

Nonetheless, that good ole boy at the hunt store in Houston said that it was definitely the weapon for him. Twelve-gauge shot gun with a something-or-other caliber bullet. Chip haggled over the price, as he knew he should. He talked the country boy down to two thousand bucks. That should prove that he was not some dumb city dude.

So Friday, he practiced with his shotgun. He lined up bean cans on a stump. Worked 'til he could stand almost twenty feet away from his target. Friday night he drank a twelve pack. He hadn't done that since college. No one needed to know he'd puked up most of the beer in the bushes beyond his campsite. But drinking and hunting were the manly thing to do.

Then Saturday morning, albeit late Saturday morning, he finally pulled on his camouflage gear, which he'd also purchased at the Houston hunt store. He loaded up his rifle, smeared bug repellent over his face, and started to stalk his prey.

Around mid-afternoon, he stopped to munch on a sports bar. Nasty things, he'd come to realize, sports bars. Not very filling, either. As he was biting into the last one, he caught sight of movement near the road that led out of the deer lease. Quickly he shoved his health bar in his pocket, mounted the shotgun against his shoulder, aimed in the general direction of the motion and squeezed the trigger.

In a hurry to get off his round, he forgot to brace himself against the kick of the weapon. He landed on his backside, which was still sore from the same gymnastic exercise of the day before. He'd just managed to crawl to his knees when the dog came racing across the field at him.

The dog was big, its body like a German Shepherd's. Its face was all teeth and jowls.

Chip had barely enough time to get to his feet and scramble onto the small scrap of a building that stood alone in the center of the field. He never would have guessed that he'd've had enough strength to pull himself up onto the seven-foot-tall wood structure, but he figured fear must do that to a man.

He was afraid for his life.

The stupid dog stayed beneath him for at least thirty minutes, biting and jumping at the shack's rotted wood. The animal made itself sick and finally limped off, disappearing into the brush. Chip, despite the realization that he'd found refuge on the top of an old outhouse, stayed there another half hour, just in case that beast came back.

Apparently, he'd nicked the dog with his shot, Chip figured as his heart rate returned to normal. The dog had been covered in blood. He wished he had his gun on the roof. He would have been dead on the target the second time.

The rest of the weekend, Chip hunted as far away from the road as possible. And he kept looking over his shoulder for that damn dog. That was how he came to fall in the creek last night when he was heading back to his base camp. He was certain, as he got closer to the camp, that he would run into that animal again. Every snap of a twig and rustle of a leaf kept him jumping and crouching in fear. About ten last evening, his final jump landed him in a muddy mess of green scum.

He went to bed drunk, for the third night in a row. And hungry. He'd eaten all of his food Friday night, thinking he'd have his kill to eat Saturday night.

The worst of it came when he awakened late this morning. His clothes were covered in green scum. Worse, those little red ants that were probably used to torture heretics in the Spanish Inquisition had found the remains of the sports bar in his clothes and decided to colonize on the spot.

He threw his clothes, ants and all, into a creek, scrubbed them best as he could while avoiding the angry ants, sure that at any moment a snake was going to bite his backside. Then he hung his clothes out on the bushes and took refuge in his sleeping bag until they dried.

The weekend was ruined, all because of that mongrel.

Which was why, as he sat there in his sleeping bag on the cement slab of what used to be a homestead, sipping at the last dregs of his tepid tea, he was horrified to hear a dog's bark coming his way. He jumped to his feet, battling to keep the sleeping bag around his middle without falling over. He hopped over to his refuge—the outhouse—and grabbed a finger hold on the half-moon carved in its side.

Then he realized his greatest fear had returned. The same dog materialized at the edge of his camp. Chip gave up trying to keep the sleeping bag at his middle, and scrambled, naked, onto the top of the outhouse.

To his relief, the dog ignored him and his campsite. It ran to the other side of the clearing and disappeared into the brush.

Chip began to crawl down from his perch when a breathless redhead, short but definitely stacked, appeared from the rise of bushes where his clothes were laid out to dry.

Barely sparing him a glance, she disappeared into the brush after the barking dog.

Stunned into paralysis, Chip waited a moment before chancing to come down from the roof again. He dangled a leg over the side when a man, jean-clad and wearing a clerical collar, came bursting forth from the bushes.

Chip froze as the man paused, looking for something. The preacher turned a questioning gaze at Chip. Understanding the query, Chip pointed in the direction the dog and woman had gone.

The pastor had barely cleared the grass when a man dressed in full sheriff's uniform burst through the bushes. "Which way?" he demanded.

Buck naked and white as a sheet, Chip cupped his hands over his privates and nodded with his head. "They went that way," he said.

He could have sworn he heard the sheriff mutter "Damned Yankee," before he disappeared in the brush, but Chip didn't take the time to let the words register as an insult.

He jumped from the outhouse roof and grabbed his sleeping bag, then his wallet. He didn't care if he had to hop all the way to Houston; he was getting the hell out of this god-forsaken state.

Suddenly he heard a woman scream high and loud. The sound scared flocks of birds from the bushes and sent ducks squawking across the swamp. The scream came from the direction in which the dog, the redhead, the preacher and the sheriff had disappeared.

This place was full of loonies, Chip Carouthers decided as he hopped toward the road. He was out of here.

Chapter Nine
What We Have Here . . .

"Twenty-four hours. At least." Sheriff James W. Novak stared down at the bloodied, cold body of Maeve O'Day, his voice quiet now that Angie's screams had subsided.

Maeve O'Day might have been a beautiful woman, Matt Hayden decided as he studied the corpse. Her hair, though mostly gray, was thick and wavy.

Those things were hard to see when her skin was gray and the look frozen on her sunken face was one of horrific agony.

Mercifully, James W. had at least closed the old woman's eyes.

Matt turned to Angie. She sat on a nearby stump, Shadow at her knee. Her first reaction of horror had given way to stunned grief. Her arms hung at her sides as if no life was in them. Her eyes stared sightlessly at her mother's body.

"A lot of blood here." James W. gestured to the knee-high grass around the body. "Probably survived the gunshot, but not the loss of blood." He raised his head as his deputy, Richard

Dube, broke through the bushes. The deputy carried a black plastic sheet under his arm, and Matt knew then that James W. had been expecting the worst all along.

Wordlessly the deputy handed the sheet to the sheriff, and James W. unfolded the cover and placed it over Maeve O'Day.

Out of sight definitely did not put the bloodied corpse out of mind, Matt decided.

"Call the coroner, Richard," James W. said quietly. "Gotta autopsy this one."

Richard, too tall and too thin to be of much help in the policing field in Matt's estimation, looked relieved to have a reason to leave the bloodied scene. If Matt guessed right, the young deputy would be tossing his cookies before he ever made it back to James W.'s green Dodge.

"The blood type'll match what we found on Shadow," James W. continued. "I'll bet the ranch on that." He raised his head and gazed at Angie. "I'm sure sorry about this, Angie."

Angie blinked as if she didn't recognize her name at first. As she stared at the black sheet covering Maeve O'Day, Matt knew she could still see the decayed condition of her mother's face. Angie swallowed hard, then focused on the sheriff. "Who would've brought her out here?"

James W. walked over to her and knelt down. "Angie, I don't think anybody brought your mamma out here. This was a horrible thing, honey, but there doesn't seem to be any foul play here."

Matt stepped forward, but James W. held him off with a sharp stare. "Eight miles out ain't too far for a person to wander when they're lost. Your mamma spent most of the last coupla years lost. In her head."

"You're sayin' this was an accident?" Angie's voice was quiet, but the look in her eye was lethal.

"Angie, we both saw that Yankee. Looked a damned fool if ever I saw one. That don't make him a murderer." James W. stood and placed his hand on Angie's shoulder. "Your mamma was in the wrong place at the wrong time, is all."

"Somebody poisoned Shadow," she pointed out.

The sheriff shook his head. "There's no tellin' what that dog coulda got into. Do you know how many tool sheds and farm buildings are between here and Wilks?"

"What about the preacher saying Mamma was in a car?" Angie pleaded.

"Shadow's not a purebred bloodhound. Of course he had trouble following Maeve's scent. Now, pastors know preachin'," James W. said and stared hard at Matt. "I know police work."

Matt held James W.'s gaze for a long moment. The threat in the sheriff's eye was clear. Matt nodded, quietly agreeing to save his argument for later.

"Angie, you need to get out of here." The new voice came from behind, and the three turned to find Bo, the ice house bartender, standing behind them. "You've seen enough."

Angie swallowed hard and shook off a chill that had nothing to do with the weather blowing in from the north. "I don't want to leave her," she whispered when she could.

"She ain't here," Bo said firmly. He looked at the tarp

covering Maeve O'Day's remains. "And Angie, you shouldn't be here either. Let the cops do their work."

The matter settled, Bo stepped forward and took Angie's elbow. She struggled to her feet. "When will Mamma's body be released?"

James W. took Angie's other arm to help steady her. "I'll call you, Angie. You go home. Warm up. As soon as the coroner gives me an idea, I'll let you know."

She nodded, took two steps, then turned back and looked at Matt. "James W. might not want to hear what you have to say, but I do, Preacher. I'll be talking to you later."

Matt nodded, then watched her disappear with Bo and Shadow into the woods.

Chapter Ten
His Mom's Pride and Joy

"I guess you've got something to say, Preacher." Sheriff James W. Novak slapped his hat on his head. The gesture did little to protect him from the spikes of rain that had begun to stab from the sky.

Pastor Matt Hayden kicked off the tree he'd been leaning against for shelter while the sheriff had gone about the business of recording death. He'd watched as the sheriff measured distances, took photographs and documented the death of Maeve O'Day. He gave a handkerchief to Richard Dube so the deputy could wipe a drop of swill off his face. Finally, he'd lent a hand to lift Maeve O'Day's body into the back of the ambulance.

"This ain't a crime scene, Preacher." James W. walked side by side with Matt back to his Dodge, which Deputy Dube had driven to the nearby clearing.

"Didn't say this was the crime scene," Matt said as he climbed into the cab. He wiped the rain from his face and turned full on the sheriff. "The crime scene is back in Wilks."

James W. took off his hat and ran a hand over his burr. "Preacher, I like you a lot. But this ain't your territory."

"James W.—"

The sheriff held up his hand. "People need your kind. Quiet-like. Peaceful. You shouldn't be ashamed of that."

Matt stared hard at the sheriff. In that moment of silence a stiff wind rocked the cab, sending a sheet of loud rain against the windshield. "Ashamed?"

James W. smiled at Matt. "No offense, Preacher. But you're kind of the passive type. And that's good," he added quickly when he saw Matt's anger flare. "But tryin' to dig up problems where none exist ain't the way to get people to respect you."

Matt held his temper in check. It took a few swallows to do so. "People don't respect me," he repeated.

"Sure they do, Preacher," James W. said quickly. "A lot of folk saw you take that punch from Angie." He let his gaze wander out to the front of the cab where heavy, black roiled in the sky. "Now you're tryin' to impress us with how much you know."

"You think I'm embarrassed because Angie decked me?"

The sheriff chuckled. "She sure did."

Matt strove for control. For him, taking that punch from Angie had been the most caring thing he could do for her at the time.

"You let people push you around sometimes," James W. said. "I know Elsbeth tore you a new one about going over to Angie's on Friday for lunch."

"I see."

James W. cleared his throat uncomfortably. He turned the ignition of his truck. "Might as well head home."

"You can drop me at the parsonage." Matt kept his tone flat.

"Now, Preacher, don't get your feathers up. I'm only tryin' to sort out what I've got before me. What happened to Maeve was an accident."

Matt held up his hands in surrender, then folded them in his lap for prayer. Prayer, he knew, was the only thing that would keep him in check at that moment. He'd learned that pretty fast after his own father had been killed.

"Lackin' further evidence—" James W. drew a steadying breath—"I have to toe the line on this one." James W. peered at Matt before turning onto the dirt road that led from the deer lease. "No hard feelin's?"

"You're making a mistake, James W. About Maeve O'Day's cause of death, anyway. As for me—" Matt had gained enough control to offer a smile. "I guess maybe I'm just a good listener. If that makes me a wimp—" He shrugged, but this time his smile was genuine. "My mom would be pleasantly surprised."

Chapter Eleven
Ernie Masterson

The Sinclair station owner considered himself a good-looking man. At fifty-five, Ernie Masterson maintained his light brown hair without the aid of a tube, and he kept his five-foot-ten frame fairly free of a beer belly. His best attribute was his eyes, however. Not only were they green . . . which the women loved . . . but they didn't miss a thing. He knew pretty much everything that went on in Wilks. He liked making people nervous. Nobody in town dared consider him a simple grease monkey. Not if they wanted their secrets to remain secrets, anyway.

His station was ideally located just off the town square, allowing him a perfect view of all of the comings and goings of the citizens of Wilks. He'd been every intentional in choosing this spot.

On his right, Ernie could see all four sides of the town square. On the far side of the square, just beyond the Muster Tree, sat Miss Olivia's mansion. He chuckled. Every time the old woman looked out her front window, she saw his Sinclair Station and fretted over her property values.

To his left, he had a full view of Angie's place, the Colorado River and Grace Lutheran Church. The parishioners still hadn't figured out he had a birds eye view of every person that came and went from that place, and not just the ones who came for Bible Studies. Ernie had picked up on more than one marriage that was in trouble when the couple came in for counselling.

It was just about twenty-four hours since Maeve O'Day had been found dead on his property, and the questions he'd had to answer about that damn Yankee renting his deer lease had taken up most of the morning. Now the sun was setting, and it was time for him to get a drink. He passed Warren Yeck's broken-down '75 pea-green Chevy as he headed out. The car had been an eyesore, rotting in the garage side yard for ten years now. He smiled. He loved the idea that he was personally bringing down the property values on the home of that old witch.

He crossed Mason Street to put in his nightly appearance at the Fire and Ice House. He liked the fact his Sinclair was right across from the local bar. He reveled in the fact that the Ice House was in such close proximity to Miss Olivia's mansion across the square.

Ernie chuckled. Miss Olivia must do a slow burn every time she walked out her front door.

Ernie stood in front of the Ice House when he saw a familiar figure walking across the Colorado River Bridge. "Hey there,

Pastor," he said, his grin wide at being caught going in for his nightly happy hour.

"Ernie." Pastor Matt Hayden greeted him, deciding not to offer a handshake when he saw the grease layered thick across the man's palm.

As they stood there, a neon Budweiser light popped on in the Fire and Ice House front window. "They're open today?" Matt asked in surprise.

Ernie shrugged. "Town still gets thirsty."

Matt considered that. The day after Maeve O'Day had been found dead, Angie had decided to keep the Fire and Ice House open.

He forgot the letter that he was going to post and followed Ernie into the Ice House.

The bar looked as it always had—neon lights reflecting in the mirror behind the bar, low-hung fluorescent tubes casting white glows on the tattered pool tables. The corner juke bubbled bright yellow and orange water, while the ceiling over the bar and dance floor glittered with small Christmas lights.

Despite the look of the place, however, the mood in the Fire and Ice House was subdued. Bo was behind the bar in his usual black T-shirt, but now the bandanna and jeans that he wore were black as well. The song coming from the jukebox was a mournful Willie Nelson singing about Georgia. The patrons talked in hushed voices such that the total of the noise in the place was surprisingly quiet.

"Mind if I join you?" Matt asked of Ernie.

A flash of surprise showed on the garage owner's face, but

he let it slide into a knowing sneer. Dirt on a pastor was the best kind of dirt. And a single man who drank was an interesting view of the man who had come so piously to Wilks. "Sure, Pastor. If you want."

The two men sat at the booth nearest the bar. "Let me buy the first round, Pastor," Ernie said jovially, then raised a hand in Bo's direction.

Bo didn't answer Ernie's call. Angie O'Day, dressed in a black T-shirt and blue jeans, her hair swept back in a black bandanna, came through the kitchen swinging doors and caught sight of Ernie's signal.

She sent a glare in Ernie's direction, then noted with surprise the fact that Matt sat across from him. Curious, she walked up to the booth. "What're you doin' here?"

Matt noted happily that her tone toward him was no longer filled with contempt. Rather, she almost seemed relieved to see him. "Thought I'd check on how you were doing. I didn't realize you'd be open today."

Angie shrugged. "People still have to eat."

Matt looked at Bo behind the bar, and noted that Dorothy Jo was working in the kitchen as well. He nodded. "Crowded for a Monday, isn't it?"

Angie grimaced. "Murder brings out curiosity seekers, I guess."

"Murder?" Ernie repeated.

Angie scowled. "That's what I call it."

Matt saw Angie's anger flare and quickly moved to diffuse it. "Two drafts, huh, Ernie?"

Ernie and Angie both turned surprised gazes his way.

"Sure, Preacher." Ernie let a grin settle on his face as Angie walked away. "You a drinkin', man, Preacher?"

"Like Martin Luther, I appreciate an occasional beer," Matt said, immediately realizing his retort sounded more defensive than he'd intended.

"Sure," Ernie agreed, warmly. His gaze quickly turned curious. "So do you think Maeve O'Day was murdered?"

Matt did indeed believe it was murder, but he didn't want to state it so blatantly. "In any case, it was a tragedy."

Ernie nodded his head. "I've never rented to a Yankee before. That Carouthers fellow was about as sharp as mashed potatoes, but he had more money than God. I thought it was a joke leasin' him the land, but a joke I'd make money on."

Matt studied Ernie, weighing whether the mechanic felt any remorse about renting to the inexperienced hunter.

"If I had thought someone would get hurt . . ." Ernie shook his head. "Hell, I've been rentin' out that property since I got it from Miss Olivia in 1980. Ain't never had anything like this happen before." Ernie slipped a pack of Camels out of his pocket and tapped one out. "Guess I missed all of the excitement yesterday." He lit a cigarette and blew out a puff of smoke. "I got there after all the shootin' was over."

"Here you go, Preacher."

Matt looked up to see Bo standing beside the table with two frosted mugs on a corked tray. Matt's gaze passed beyond to watch Angie dab at her eyes before disappearing into the kitchen.

"Thanks." Matt waited for Bo to place the drinks on the table. "Is Angie okay?"

Bo looked in the direction of the kitchen. "No," he answered.

"Maybe I'll talk to her in a little bit."

Bo gave a slight nod to the pastor, glared hard at the gas station owner and walked back to the bar.

Matt turned his attention back to Ernie. "So how did Carouthers come to find out you had land to lease?"

"Got a website." Ernie took a long chug at his beer, draining a third of the glass. "Call came in on Christmas Eve, of all things. Had the whole family over for doin's. I charged Carouthers three times the lease just for callin' on a holiday. He paid up without a grunt. We toasted the stupid jerk." He offered a small smile in Matt's direction. "You should try Elsbeth's wassail sometimes. Has a great kick."

"I'll keep that in mind."

Ernie stuck his cigarette in his lips and lit it. "Even Miss Olivia got a chuckle over the deal."

"How is it that you all spend your holidays together?" Matt asked, taking his first sip of beer.

"Pearl was married to Roth. You know, James W.'s older brother. The one that died in Iran."

Matt sat back, surprised. "Really."

"Didn't you know? Heck, I figured you pastors looked all of that stuff up in church records before you preached your first sermon." Ernie was pleased at his ability to be the source of news to the pastor. Pastors, in his estimation, knew almost as much gossip as he did. "Pearl and Roth were hitched a few months before he went over to rescue them hostages. Roth never came back. Sand storm, my ass."

The Iranian hostage crisis? Matt would have to check into that. "Hard time for the country. Can't imagine what it would've been like for Miss Olivia."

"Yeah. I was glad I could help Miss Olivia out."

Matt arched his eyebrow. "What do you mean?"

"Miss Olivia was all upset about Roth, then Cash." He chuckled to himself and took another chug from his beer. "She was sure upset about Cash."

"He was her husband."

Ernie smirked. "You don't know the half of it." He wiped the frost of the beer away from his mouth. "Anyway, she didn't want to be stuck with takin' care of Pearl. She let it be known to me that she'd appreciate it if I could 'handle' the situation, as they say."

Matt took a moment to register Ernie's meaning. "Is that how you came into the Novak land?"

Ernie grinned. "I like you, Preacher. I really do. I got that and a few other things." He shrugged. "What the heck? Pearl was used goods. And I sure got Miss Olivia out of a jam."

Matt kept his gaze friendly, but in his estimation Ernie had just crossed a line with him. "It's a wonder Pearl was agreeable to another marriage after losing her husband."

Ernie shrugged. "She had a duty. She didn't want to be a burden to Miss Olivia. After all, Miss Olivia lost a son and a husband."

"Literally lost a husband, I understand," Matt said. "Cash Novak's body was never found?"

Ernie nodded, shifted. "Cash was in Houston for the presidential debate. He was busier than a three-legged cat tryin' to cover up poop on an icy pond."

"Cash was in politics?"

"He had money and he had opinions, and with him bein' in the army twice, he sure as hell had connections. But I found him. Got word to him that Roth was dead. He headed home." Ernie took a drag. "But he never made it. First place I went lookin' for that crazy sonuvagun was Miss Lida's."

"The whorehouse?" Matt's head came up in surprise.

"So you heard about that place, huh?" Ernie grinned. "Cash and I went there occasionally. Lord knows he wasn't gettin' any at home."

Ernie lifted his hand to order another beer, but Matt knew he had heard all he could tolerate. He stood and threw a couple of dollars on the table. "Thanks for the time, Ernie. I'm gonna see how Angie's doing."

Without a backward glance, Matt walked into the kitchen.

"Done drinkin' with the devil?"

If Matt had been expecting tears, he should have known better. Angie O'Day was standing over the fryer, her face red from the hot grease of the sputtering fries.

Instead of answering her, Matt went over to the porcelain sink labeled "Hand Washing Only" and ran his hands under hot water.

"Feelin' greasy, Preacher?" she challenged. "Hangin' out

with slime like Ernie'll do that to you. More often than not Bo has to take him home 'cuz Ernie's too drunk to find the way himself, and the man only lives across the street."

Matt flicked a paper towel from the dispenser above the sink and dried his hands. Angie was right, actually. Being around Ernie Masterson left him feeling soiled. "How are you doing, Angie?"

"Couldn't be better," she said, raising a basket full of fries from the grease and dumping them in a paper-lined pan. She picked up a shaker and began salting the fries. "My mother's dead because someone drove her out to a deer lease and let her loose, and the sheriff says it was an accident."

"You blame Ernie."

"I hate Ernie," she corrected him. "I blame the sheriff for not seein' the evidence right in front of him."

Matt swallowed uncomfortably. His words about Shadow had put the thought in Angie's mind that Maeve had been driven to her death.

"Hate's a strong word."

"As much grief as Ernie has given me about growing into a 'beautiful woman' all the while eyein' my breasts like they would be his next lunch, makes a woman consider hate. That's a pervert sittin' out there, Preacher." She pointed accusingly at the swinging doors. "He goes to your church."

"Angie." Matt cleared his throat.

"To think, I was afraid once that he was my father. As much as he hung around my mamma, talkin' to her in private." She shook her head, all the while liberally salting the fries. "Mamma laughed when I asked her. Out and out belly-laughed."

"Angie?" Matt stepped forward.

"Mamma had a wonderful laugh. She said me bein' afraid Ernie was my father was the funniest thing she ever heard."

"Angie." Matt cleared his throat.

"Then she slapped me for thinkin' she'd go to bed with a man like that."

"Angie?"

"What?" she demanded impatiently, slamming the saltshaker on the table. "I'm tellin' you my life story here."

"Angie, are you expecting people to eat those fries?"

The preacher tried not to laugh. She could see it in the way his lips twitched. She looked down at the mound of fries that were now coated with a thick blanket of salt.

She swallowed down her embarrassment. "Salt makes people drink more," she muttered. "Good for business."

Matt allowed her answer to pass without comment, even when she dumped the fries into the garbage and went to the freezer to pull out another bag.

"So Maeve never told you who your father is?"

Angie slit open the plastic bag of fries and poured them into the wire mesh basket. She lowered them into the hot grease. "Nope," she answered finally.

"Why?"

"Because she'd made a promise, and Maeve O'Day never breaks a promise." Angie swallowed hard. "Never broke a promise," she corrected herself.

Then finally, because she'd fought it off for so long, and

maybe because someone was there who cared enough to ask how she was doing, Angie O'Day sat down on the three-legged stool by the stove and cried.

"Angie," Matt said quietly. "You shouldn't be here tonight." He crossed to where she sat sobbing, momentarily fought a desire to place an arm around her shoulder, then gave in. Her shoulders were smaller than he'd expected. More feminine. He shook his head against the thought. "Bo and Dorothy Jo can handle things down here."

"I have to keep it goin'. The place. It's her."

"It's both of you," Matt said. "It won't go belly-up if you're not here for one night."

"She would have been here." Angie wiped at her wet face, then walked to the counter where she swiped a paper towel from the dispenser.

"She would do what she needed to do. You need to do what you need to do."

Swollen-eyed, Angie looked back at him. "You're startin' to sound like a preacher again."

Matt took a deep breath. "I'll risk a little more, then. Have you made all of the arrangements? For the funeral and all?"

"The coroner released Mamma's body to the funeral home today. We won't be havin' an open casket."

The condition of the body precluded that, Matt already knew. The bitterness in Angie's voice was understandable. "When's the service?"

"Tomorrow. One o'clock." A new tear streaked down her cheek.

"Angie, I'd be honored if you'd let me say a few words at your mother's funeral."

Angie looked up at him in surprise. "She was Catholic."

"She was Christian," Matt said quietly. "At least that's what it sounds like from what you've told me."

"She was. More Christian than most—" Angie stopped in mid-sentence.

Matt smiled sadly. "Than most of my parishioners?"

Angie nodded, refusing to feel sheepish.

"I would like to be of help to you. That's what I think being a Christian is about."

Angie looked at him sharply. "You and Mamma got more in common than I realized." Finally, she shook her head. "You're buyin' yourself a lot of problems, Preacher."

"Some people think I'm a wimp, Angie. This is my way of being strong."

Angie stood. "I'll talk to the priest." She gave Matt a hug. "Thanks," she whispered. She was about to break the hug when a leering voice came from the doorway.

"A word of advice," Ernie Masterson said. He was leaning against the doorjamb, one ankle kicked over the other. His green eyes looked delighted at what he saw. "I wouldn't do that in full view of the bar."

Angie pulled away from the preacher and turned full on Ernie.

"I've put up with you bein' a pervert and a drunk, Ernie Masterson. But I won't put up with you turnin' sympathy for my mamma's dyin' into something dirty." Angie picked up a butcher knife and stalked toward him. "Get the hell outta my bar."

"You're gettin' your Irish up, Angie girl," Ernie said, backing up. The amusement drained from his face.

"It's Angie ma'am to you from now on," she said, her pace toward him steady. "If you ever step foot in my bar again, I'll take care of you so you'll never be a perverted drunk again. Understand?"

"Angie, I'm one of your best customers." Ernie let the swinging doors go as he backed into the bar, but Angie punched through them, knife first.

"Not anymore you ain't. My mamma's dead because you let some Yankee loose on your property with a loaded gun. I'm never gonna forget it, Ernie Masterson. Or forgive you."

Ernie backed around the bar. Matt followed through the kitchen doors.

"You owe ten bucks, Masterson." Bo came around the other end of the U-shaped bar and grabbed Ernie by the collar. "I'll pay this round 'cuz I'm never gonna have to serve your sorry ass again," Bo said, his face flushed with anger. "See that you treat your missus real good from now on, or Angie and I'll both come after you."

Bo kicked at the front door, and with what looked to Matt like a great deal of pleasure, threw Ernie Masterson out on to Mason Street.

Matt swallowed hard as the door slammed shut. He told himself it had simply been a typical bar brawl. No sheriff called. No blood spilled. Probably the only casualty in the place was the lining of his stomach.

Then he noted that the bar was completely silent. Not a beer was being lifted. Not a cue ball shot.

Every eye in the place was trained on him where he stood in the doorway between kitchen and bar.

Angie finally let the knife drop from violent threat to dead weight at her side. She turned toward the kitchen. "You sure have a way of stirrin' things up," she said under her breath as she passed by Matt.

She walked to the fryer, hauled out the cooked batch of fries, and dumped them into a paper-lined tray.

Chapter Twelve
Ancestry.Ben

"She's deader than a doornail, Reverend." Warren Yeck helplessly kicked at the front tire of the church's blue Ford Aerostar van. Matt had been too jumpy after the scene in Angie's bar to go straight home. He'd seen the light on in the Yecks' store's loading dock and decided to stop by and learn how the church's van was faring. Its motor had died halfway up 71 on the trek to find Angie's mother.

The van was parked beneath a sign announcing the store's name—Yeck's Seed, Feed and Hardware Needs. Most folks simply called it the SF & H Store. Ben Yeck, Warren's younger brother by two years, pushed out from under the vehicle's hood. "Doubt if even Ernie can fix this."

Matt leaned against the doorjamb of the brothers' garage. "I don't suppose there's any money in the budget for a replacement?"

"There ain't even money in the budget to fix it." Ben slammed the hood shut.

Warren nodded. "I'll call Ernie in the morning." He turned at the sound of a buzzer going off on his watch. "That's the cabbage rolls," he said, then disappeared to the outside stairs that led to the small apartment the brothers had shared for ten years.

Ben's face brightened. "Cabbage rolls. My favorite. Care to stay for dinner?"

"Thanks, Ben. Not tonight. Sounds delicious, though." Matt tried his best not to grimace at the sound of the dish.

"Cabbage rolls are a Czech specialty. That's what we are, you know. Czech. Our last name is really Yelvetichek. I'll wager the man at Ellis Island who let my grandpappy in was havin' a bad day and came up with 'Yeck'."

Matt kept his tongue in his cheek as he tried not to smile too broadly at Ben's musings. "So what's wrong with the van?"

"My money's on the electrical system," Ben said, wiping the grease off his hands.

Matt grimaced. He'd hoped to use the church van if his Ford went belly-up as well. "I guess taking it out to find Maeve was too much for it."

Ben nodded his whistle-clean, bald head. Matt noted that the years of working the SF & H's counter had been kinder to Ben's skin than the seasons Warren had spent on his tractor beneath the hot Texas sun. "Maeve was a nice lady. No matter what you might've heard."

"I've heard otherwise, that's for sure." Matt followed Ben out of the garage. He waited as Ben fumbled for his keys.

"How do you think Maeve got out there?" Ben queried. He

was by far the more astute of the two brothers, Matt realized. Probably from the years of running his own store.

"Seemed to me it would have been too far for her to walk." Matt shrugged. "The sheriff feels otherwise."

Ben shook his head. "Maybe five years ago Maeve could've walked it. But that Alzheimer's had her pretty feeble."

Matt nodded. He'd surmised as much from what he'd already heard.

"Somebody drove her out there," Ben said. With a shake of his head, he headed for the back stairs that led to the apartment above the Seed, Feed and Hardware Needs store.

"So it would seem." Matt looked up as a bolt of lightning split the sky overhead. "Any ideas who would do a thing like that?"

Ben thought for a long moment before answering. "Mebbe."

They'd reached the bottom of the stairs. It had been a long evening already, Matt thought wearily, and it wasn't over. Ben had something to say, and unlike his brother who would give a history lesson at a moment's notice, he took his time in choosing his words.

"Maeve worked at a pony house," Ben finally said.

Matt nodded. "That's what I heard."

"She was the bartender," Ben said with finality, and Matt knew better than to question how Ben had come about that bit of information.

"That was over thirty years ago," Matt observed.

Ben nodded. "You learn a lot of secrets when you tend a bar. Sometimes it's like runnin' a confessional."

"Sounds like you've done a bit of bartending yourself."

"Warren worked the Officer's Club over in Killen during Viet Nam. He heard a lot of things he never wanted to know."

"So you're saying maybe Maeve heard some things at Lida's Rose Hotel that she shouldn't have."

"Somethin' like that."

"What does that have to do with now?"

"Now, she was an old lady with Alzheimer's. Who didn't remember what she wasn't supposed to repeat, maybe."

Matt nodded slowly. It made sense. "So, who . . .?"

"Who knew there was a dumb Yankee on that deer lease yesterday?"

"Ernie." Matt let out a breath. First Angie, now Ben was thinking that Ernie was involved.

"I'm not sayin'. It's none of my business."

"Did Ernie go to Lida's Rose Hotel?"

Ben Yeck let out a hearty laugh. "Ernie followed Cash Novak around like a puppy dog. Wherever Cash went, Ernie went."

"Ernie idolized Cash."

"Everything about him. His sense of humor. His sense of money. The man was twenty years Ernie's senior, but they hung together like Mutt and Jeff."

"And Cash frequented Lida's Rose Hotel."

Ben let out another chuckle. "Kept her in business, as far as I'm concerned. You don't think it was a coincidence that she got closed down just a month after Cash disappeared, do you?"

"Ben! You comin'?" Warren called from upstairs.

Matt shook Ben's hand, then headed out past the dormant redbuds that separated the SF & H store's property from the church. He had a lot of praying to do.

After all, Ernie Masterson was a parishioner.

Chapter Thirteen
The Guest at the Funeral

The next morning, Pastor Matt Hayden pulled his black suit coat off the hook by his office door and shrugged into it. "I'll be back in a few hours."

"It's real nice, you goin' to that funeral, Reverend," said Ann Fullenweider. The efficient church secretary gave him an approving nod that bobbed the pearl barrette in her jet-black hair. "It's the Christian thing to do."

"Thank you, Mrs. Fullenweider," Matt said, somewhat uncomfortable with the action he was about to take. "There are those in this church who will not agree with you, I'm sure."

She huffed out a breath. "The Wilks and Novaks," she said, shaking her head. "That bunch—well, they like huggin' rosebushes, is all I can say."

Matt smiled inwardly. Perhaps one of the things he liked best about the capable Mrs. Fullenweider was her take on the realities of Grace Lutheran Church. She certainly had experience at the job, he knew. She'd started as the church

secretary thirty years earlier—two years before Pastor Osterburg
had finished his tenure at Grace Lutheran.

"Pastor Osterburg!" Matt said suddenly.

"Beg pardon, Reverend?" Ann asked.

"I have a letter I'm supposed to mail to him. I promised him
I'd write and tell him how things were going after I settled in."

Mrs. Fullenweider smiled, bright red lips revealing well-
fitted dentures. "I hope you sent my hello to him."

"I did indeed." Matt smiled back. His secretary might have
used a bit too much make-up and a tad too dark hair dye, but
her heart was pure gold. "Mrs. Fullenweider?"

"Yes, Reverend?"

"I was wondering, with the funeral and all . . ."

"Yes, Reverend?"

Matt leaned against the wall. "Do you know much about
Ernie Masterson?"

For the first time since Matt had been at Grace, Ann
Fullenweider scowled.

"I know enough," she said shortly. She arched a thickly
penciled eyebrow at him. "I take it since you're askin', you
know about my family and Ernie Masterson."

Matt shrugged. "No."

She snorted. "You might say our families aren't on
borrowing terms."

"Why?"

"I'll tell you." The secretary's gaze turned angry. "Ernie
pumped gas for my daughter the day she and her husband split.
It wasn't a big fight. Probably something they could've made

up over." She shook her head. "Not with Ernie Masterson's mouth, though. Before she was on my doorstep, Ernie had told half the town those two were getting a divorce."

"That soured any reconciliation."

"You bet it did. Zach Gibbons, my daughter's ex, he was a proud man. With word out that his wife left him . . . well, he wasn't gonna take her back without an apology. She had nothing to apologize for."

"Why did she leave him?"

"Zach's drinking!" Mrs. Fullenweider said indignantly. "Ain't no way Sarah was gonna put up with that."

"You think Ernie was the final straw."

"I know Ernie was the final straw, Reverend. Sarah said she was going to go back the next day after Zach sobered up. She was going to have one of those in-ter-ven-tions with him."

Matt nodded. He was familiar with the process of confronting an addict with his or her problem.

"She had everyone lined up. Zach's parents, the pastor, a coworker. But no. Thanks to Ernie, Zach wouldn't see any of 'em. He filed for divorce against Sarah on the grounds of desertion, and got their son to boot! With Texas being a common property state, all my daughter got was a five-acre lot outside of town and a life full of grief."

Matt let out a sigh. "I'm sorry. I didn't know."

"That's all right, Pastor." She calmed her breathing, took her purse from her desk's bottom drawer, removed her compact and powdered her nose. "You didn't know. Ernie made a lot of enemies on that one, and my daughter's only one example of the havoc that man wreaks in people's lives around here."

"He has a lot of enemies."

"You can put Zach Gibbons at the top of that list." She smiled smugly. "He'll never admit it, but I'll bet you money Zach is the one who burned down Ernie's house out on the old Novak property."

Matt's head came up. "Where Maeve O'Day was found?"

"There were antiques aplenty in that place, I can tell you. Used to be a real nice spread. Now all that's left is the outhouse."

Matt remembered a vision of Chip Carouthers perched on the top of that outhouse and smothered a grin. "No love lost between Zach and Ernie, then."

"No love lost between most of this town and Ernie Masterson," Mrs. Fullenweider said. "After all the tears that man caused my daughter—" She turned back to addressing an envelope. "I wouldn't mind taking a swipe at him myself."

**

Three hours later, Pastor Matt Hayden opened the door to the tiny room behind Grace Lutheran Church's altar and quietly walked inside.

The sacristy was a small walnut-paneled room lined with shelves to hold supplies—altar paraments, a closet for the pastoral robes, and a cupboard for the silver communion chalices. In the wall closest to the window was a small silver sink, its drain allowing unused communion wine to flow straight to the earth below, thus returning the blood of Christ to the ground immediately following the sacrament.

Matt crossed to the closet, unlocked its door and lifted the heavy bronze chain and cross from his neck. He kissed the cross before hanging it back on its nail peg just inside the closet door. The tiny looped scratches above the nail told him the nail had been used for much the same purpose by the pastors that had served Grace before him. He straightened his black suit over his black collar, checked his sandy brown hair in the mirror hanging inside the closet and shut the door, locking it in place. He let out a heavy sigh.

Maeve O'Day's funeral had been more of an ordeal than he had expected.

The crowd, numbering over one hundred and fifty, had crammed into the wooden pews of the Roman Catholic Church. Five miles off Interstate 10 and only twenty minutes from Wilks, the church was on the Texas historical record as one of its celebrated painted churches.

The people gathered today for Maeve's funeral, however, didn't bother to look at the famous ceiling. They cast their gazes downward, the hardwood floor of the church of more interest than the Catholic priest who presided over the service, or for that matter, the Lutheran minister who said a prayer at the end.

The sorrow in the church had been heavy, the air laden with quiet sobs and gentle murmurings. Angie O'Day sat in the front pew next to Dorothy Jo Devereaux, only five feet away from the draped steel casket centered in the front of the church.

The fact that Maeve O'Day had been loved was obvious.

The fact that she was not, nor ever had been, a prostitute was even more clear.

One man, stooped in shoulder and shaky in step, had gotten up and talked about how Maeve had kept him fed when he'd fallen on hard times in the oil bust. Another woman spoke of how Maeve had volunteered at the Home for Unwed Mothers in New Braunfels.

Through all of the proceedings, Angie O'Day had sat in the front pew, her hair swept up and covered in a black veil. She'd worn a proper, conservative black suit. Matt noticed it, nonetheless. She'd cried some, smiled bravely at those who came to eulogize her mother, recited her rosary with a passion on her face.

More of a surprise to him, however, than the kindness of Maeve O'Day or the faith shown in Angie's face, had been the presence of one of the members from his own parish.

Elsbeth Novak.

When Matt had stood at the end of the service to pronounce the closing prayer, Elsbeth had looked as surprised to see him as he was to see her.

He'd stuttered a moment before launching ahead, bumbled again when most in the congregation made the sign of the cross when he invoked the Father, Son, and Holy Spirit, then tripped over himself trying to get to the back of the church to talk with the junior Mrs. Novak. Elsbeth, however, apparently moved quickly. By the time Matt worked his way through the mourners and outside to the hearse, Elsbeth was driving away in her Oldsmobile.

Matt closed the sacristy door behind him, walked to the front of Grace's sanctuary and sat in the front pew before the altar.

Maeve O'Day had been there for people in need. She had helped women who had found themselves in similar situations as her own—unmarried and with child. She had raised a daughter who tolerated a great deal of injustice, and who by all accounts still believed in God.

Matt looked down at his hands and saw that they were folded for prayer. He wondered what he should pray for at that moment.

Perhaps he should ask the Good Lord to help him show his congregation how to be as charitable as Maeve O'Day.

Maybe he should ask for a generous heart in dealing with Elsbeth Novak. What exactly had she been doing at Maeve's funeral, anyway?

When Matt finally dropped to his knees, however, his prayer was for one thing and one thing only.

God help him, he couldn't stop thinking about Angie O'Day.

Chapter Fourteen
Miss Olivia

"Pastor Hayden?"

Matt stopped on the well-worn brick sidewalk that ran the length of Jefferson Street across the Town Square. He'd finally remembered to mail his letter to Pastor Osterburg and decided to take the more picturesque route past the Wilks Mansion.

"Miss Olivia," he said, bowing his head in the brisk wind. He was surprised the wind didn't blow her four-foot-eight frame over as she stood up to her knees in the plants that lined the mansion's iron fence.

"Supposed to freeze tonight," Miss Olivia said by way of explanation. "I've got to cover my azaleas." In her shaking hand she held out the corner of a bed sheet.

"Let me help you," Matt said, taking the hint.

"Don't have my usual help," Miss Olivia complained, more to herself than to Matt. "Pearl had to run the office for Ernie today. Said he wasn't in the mood to deal with customers."

Matt controlled a knowing look. More likely Ernie had a

hangover wrapped around a bruised ego.

Miss Olivia grabbed up her pearl-hooked cane and leaned on it to walk a corner of the sheet over the green leafy plants. "Heaven only knows where Elsbeth is today. Probably somethin' to do with Jimmy Jr., I suppose."

Matt decided it was best not to mention Elsbeth's appearance at Maeve's funeral earlier. Whatever her reason for being there, Elsbeth apparently had not received permission from Miss Olivia to attend.

"Would you care to come in for some coffee, Reverend?" Miss Olivia asked when they had finished covering the last of the bushes.

"Sounds wonderful," Matt replied.

He followed her up the red brick sidewalk to the looming three-story Victorian home. Four white pillars fronted the plantation style portico. Black shutters framed the tall, paned windows. Beveled glass panels rimmed the doublewide carved oak doors.

The grounds took up an entire block of Jefferson Street, the house itself more than half of it. Gardens with crisp hedges and sprawling live oak trees flanked both sides of the mansion. A carriage house, complete with matching paned windows and delicate gingerbread artistry, peeked around the corner of the mansion.

Matt walked patiently as Miss Olivia made her way. He helped her up the stairs and opened the front door for her.

The smell of coffee mixed with the scent of apples and cinnamon greeted them, and a wave of familiarity rushed through him.

His mom, Jewel Hogan, had always kept a pot of coffee and some kind of pie ready for her husband and sons when they came home from being cops

"Your home is beautiful, Miss Olivia," he remarked as she pulled off her scarf and put it on the marble-topped phone table.

"Been in the family since before the War of Northern Aggression." She removed her coat and eased it over the tree horse in the corner.

Matt kept his smile to himself. Warren Yeck had treated him to the Texas view of the Civil War before.

Warren loved to tell a story.

"My granddaddy added the two side wings at the turn of the century. Plenty of room for James W. and Elsbeth. Can't imagine why they wanted to live in that ranch house." Miss Olivia took Matt's coat and put it over the antique tree that was a full two feet taller than she was.

"Children can be a challenge," Matt said.

"Jimmy Jr. already let me know he wants to settle here. That's just fine."

The matriarch seemed appeased by that. Apparently, the gubernatorial candidate had learned early in life how to play politics. Perhaps the kid had potential as governor.

Miss Olivia made her way through the parlor with its brocade rugs and Victorian furniture, past the federal blue dining room where mirrors of polished bronze hung on the muslin-covered walls.

She gestured the preacher through a swinging door, then

followed him into the kitchen. The room was dank, thought Matt in surprise as he entered what was usually the heart of most homes. The walls were painted a flat gray and the counter tops covered in an even darker gray Formica. The white refrigerator and other white appliances did little to offset the dullness of the room. In the corner by the stove, a small white dog lay sleeping on a fluffy gray dog bed.

"That's Blanco," Miss Olivia said, following the preacher's gaze. At the sound of his name, the old Havanese lifted his head and wagged his tail. Miss Olivia hooked her cane around a cookie jar on a corner shelf, lifted it down and took out a scrap of biscuit. She tossed it to the dog, then pushed the cookie jar back into place with her cane. Blanco gobbled the treat and contentedly laid his head back against the soft pillow-top.

"In dog years he's about as old as I am," Miss Olivia said and smiled. She ambled over to the old-fashioned gray coffee pot on the back burner of the stove, ignited the flame beneath the pot and turned. "Would you care for cream or sugar, Reverend Hayden?"

Realizing he was about to get the leftovers of her morning coffee, Matt mustered a smile and said, "Both, please."

"That's fine," she said and put cups and condiments on a silver tray. "We'll have our coffee in the parlor."

***

The mansion's parlor was a room of beauty, Matt decided. A public room, its ornamentation played a sharp contrast to the blandness of the kitchen.

Prisms ornamented every hand-painted shade; a crystal chandelier decorated with brass adornments hung in the center of the parlor. A grand piano stood in the corner at the front of the house, its size swallowed by the grandeur of the room. The Victorian-era furniture was cream silk with blue and red flowers. A large Oriental silk rug spun with dark blue and gold threads spanned the distance between the couch and matching chairs.

"What brought you here to Wilks?" Miss Olivia asked, bringing the cup of coffee to her wrinkled lips.

"I met a man at seminary who used to be the preacher here at Grace. Reverend Osterburg?"

The old woman's eyes lit. "He was a pillar in the community. Served here over twenty years. Confirmed me. Married me." She put down her cup. "Did the memorial service for my husband."

"He taught some of my sermon classes."

Miss Olivia nodded her approval. "He was a powerful speaker."

"When I got the call to Grace, I looked up Pastor Osterburg. He's a visiting professor at the University of St. Thomas, you know. He lobbied me pretty hard to accept." Matt silently prayed for numb taste buds as he took his first sip of coffee. "He was very persuasive."

"Bless him," Miss Olivia said. She rose from the couch and, much to his dismay, refilled Matt's cup. "We went without a full-time pastor for over two years."

"It's hard to get the rural pulpits filled." Matt nodded.

"Wilks is more than a rural town. We're the county seat!" Miss Olivia said indignantly, then immediately softened her tone. "Of course, you know that already," she added graciously. "I'm curious as to what you see your role as bein' in Wilks, Reverend."

Matt paused in his sip. "I take it there's a hint in there, somewhere, Miss Olivia."

She smiled, though the smile lacked sincerity. He felt a lecture coming on.

"In a smaller town like Wilks," she began, "everyone has more responsibility to take an interest in civic needs. That's what makes us so personable." She sat back in the couch. "A citizen in a large town has the advantage that they believe someone else will do the work. Someone usually will. Here, it's up to us."

"I see," Matt replied. He wasn't sure he saw at all.

"We must be the example to our children," Miss Olivia said. "We are the role models for them to look up to. We must do things and act in ways that are respectable. Honorable. Don't cause problems."

Matt put down his cup. "Are you referring to something specific in my actions, Miss Olivia?"

"That's for you to decide, Reverend Hayden."

Matt shifted uncomfortably. "How do you decide what is right and what is wrong, Miss Olivia?"

"That is somethin' that develops with experience. I'll tell you what I've learned." She sat straighter, a certain pride entering her posture. "A person looks around. Sees gray. Yes, gray," she repeated at his questioning look. "This action could be interpreted this way, or that person might've said that meanin' something else. Life is full of gray."

He could see from the faraway look on her face that she was thinking of a specific time in her life.

"Then you look at what it is, and what it needs to be. *Needs* to be, Pastor." She wagged her finger at him. "For the good of everyone concerned. That's when you see the black and white. You see what has to be done. You see what your duty is."

Matt considered this. Apparently, Miss Olivia did not think it was his duty to be involved in Maeve O'Day's search party or preaching about it from the pulpit. "Are you referring to my sermon on Sunday? I felt morally bound to get the town together to help find her."

"Morals!" Miss Olivia pushed away the thought with a brush of her hand. "Your morals are probably what kept you from accepting that $2,000 as a down payment for a new car."

"Actually, yes."

"What did your morals do for the common good? You're driving a car that could break down at any moment. You might be on your way to console a grieving family, or a hospital visit, and phht! You're in the middle of nowhere and can't be there for the people who'd need you." The old woman shook her head. "People make up morals to have excuses for their decisions."

"I see." This time he did see. Miss Olivia might have the good of the town at heart, but her logic was flawed. God made right. God made wrong.

"I didn't intend to get so personal," Miss Olivia said, a slight blush steeling over her pale cheeks. "When you brought up Pastor Osterburg, however, I couldn't help but remember how he took such an interest in civic matters. He went to every town council meeting. Opened them with a prayer, closed them with a benediction."

"Town council meetings?" Matt echoed. His thoughts raced. How do establishments like the Fire and Ice House become realities in such a small town? Town councils give permits. Bars require liquor licenses. Apparently, neither the Wilks nor the Novaks wanted the Fire and Ice House in town, yet here it was. How surprising. "Actually, Miss Olivia, I might find town council meetings very interesting. Why don't you tell me a little more about how government works here in Wilks?"

Chapter Fifteen
A Promise to Mamma

Angie dumped a glob of bleach into the floor drain nearest the kitchen door, then in the one by the big walk-in freezer, and again in the drain nearest the sink. The routine ended what she called her Health Department cleaning. Every month, she gave the kitchen a shine that would make Martha Stewart proud. The trouble was, she'd gone through this entire routine only two days earlier.

She looked around her kitchen. The grease in the fryer was drained, the industrial dishwasher scoured. She'd taken the shelves out of the fridge and bleached 'em down, taken the oven apart and degreased every inch of it, and even cleaned the ice machine. The kitchen was spotless.

Thinking about Mamma was the only activity left to do.

The funeral earlier had been a beautiful tribute. Angie was glad people had come out of the woodwork to say what Maeve O'Day had meant to them. Of course, they had been talking about the Maeve O'Day of twenty years ago, ten years ago.

Even six years ago. Maeve O'Day of recent times hadn't really been Maeve O'Day at all.

The glint had left Mamma's eyes, replaced with confusion. Her once-lilting voice had sunk to depressed moans and complaints. Maeve's quips of sage wisdom had given way to a blank expression. Maybe that's why Angie felt like such a traitor on this night of her mother's funeral. A part of her was glad that Maeve O'Day would no longer suffer.

Angie put the lid back on the bleach bottle, placed the bottle under the sink where she kept all of her cleaning supplies and took off her apron. She walked through the swinging doors into the bar.

"Done in there?" Bo asked.

He looked worried. Small wonder, she reckoned. She hadn't said a word since the funeral had ended when she, Bo and Dorothy Jo had returned to the bar and gone back to work.

"As done as it'll ever get." She shrugged. She looked at the Budweiser clock behind the bar. "It's only nine o'clock," she said more to herself than to Bo. "Feels like midnight."

"Why don't you head upstairs, Angie," Bo suggested. "It's quiet. If anyone wants food I can shove a pizza in the oven."

Angie looked around the Fire and Ice House. Whereas last night there had been plenty of patrons around to watch her kick Ernie Masterson out, tonight there were only three customers in the place. Two of them were regulars who sat at the bar most every Tuesday.

A thought struck her. "Any sign of Masterson tonight?"

"Not if he wants to live," Bo said, and his look was violent.

Angie understood his dislike for Ernie Masterson. Bo had taken Ernie home more than once. The last time Bo returned from such a trip, he had been hosting a bloodied lip.

"Don't beat me to it," Angie said wryly. A streak of lightning blazed outside the front window and Angie walked forward. A rumble of thunder greeted her when she reached the glass. "Gonna be a bad one, I think," she said.

"Another norther. Freeze warnin's up," Bo said. He glanced at the TV silently playing an NBA game behind him. "They've run a couple of advisories."

She nodded. "G'night, Bo." She gave the street a last look, then headed past the bar and kitchen to the very back of the Ice House.

"Hey, Angie?"

She turned. "Yeah?"

"That was a good thing you did for Dorothy Jo. About Lawrence, I mean."

Angie nodded. "She'd never wanted to get him a plot of his own. She was afraid somebody would vandalize it. Not havin' his ashes in the ground, though, I don't think Dorothy Jo could ever really put him to rest."

"Puttin' that urn on top of your mamma's casket was about the nicest thing I've ever heard of anyone doin' for somebody else."

"It was Mamma's idea years back when she first got sick. Said it wasn't right for Dorothy Jo to have to see her son's ashes on her front room bookshelf every day." Angie slapped her leg for Shadow to join her. The dog pulled himself off the brick by the wood-burning fireplace and followed her out the back door into the cold night.

The wind whipped at Angie's hair as she climbed the back steps to her small apartment. She fished a key from her jeans, unlocked the apartment's kitchen door, and headed inside. Shadow followed close behind. He went to his braided rag rug and lay down with a huff. Angie wasn't sure if the dog was in mourning or still feeling sick from the poison. Either way, she envied his ability to fall fast asleep. She shut the kitchen door.

Mamma.

The place smelled of her. The bacon she'd fried up every morning, the cedar from the chest where she kept her best linens, the after-bath that hinted at lilacs.

The kitchen was small, with barely enough room for a two-chair table, fridge and oven. Yet Maeve O'Day had cooked many a family meal in this room. Angie fingered the lace doily that topped the table. Mamma had been proud of her doilies. Said her family in Ireland had been famous for the lace they made. Angie had never met any of them.

She moved beyond the kitchen into the small living room where a faded maroon couch sat across from the triple-paned window that looked out onto Mason Street. Restless, she kept moving until she reached Maeve's small bedroom at the end of the hall. Angie went to the small Victorian walnut dresser and picked up the silver-backed brush that had been her mother's treasure. Had it been a gift from a lover? Maybe even her father? Angie stroked it through her hair. Her gaze fell on the tube of delicate-pink lipstick her mother had always worn. Smoothing it on her lips was like getting a kiss from Mamma all over again.

Everywhere was Maeve. The little touches that she had added as her small budget allowed had given Angie some semblance of a normal childhood. Maeve's had been anything but normal.

As a toddler, Maeve Catherine O'Day had come to Texas when her father was stationed at Fort Hood in 1944. A month before D-day he'd shipped out. Maeve's father had never come home.

Maeve and her mother had made do as best they could. Maeve's mother, while working as a cleaning woman at the Killeen hospital, had caught polio and died. The next year Jonas Salk's vaccine had been released to the public. Maeve O'Day, seventeen and penniless, had gone in search of a job.

Angie was pretty sure Maeve had never considered actually selling her body at Lida's Rose Hotel. Her Roman Catholic upbringing had been strong, and her backbone even stronger. Still, only the likes of Miss Lida were interested in helping a girl who was down on her luck. Miss Lida had known what that had been like. When the madam had learned that Maeve could mix a drink of whiskey and rye and not waste the liquor, Miss Lida had recognized a marketable skill in the young Irish girl. Maeve O'Day had been employed at the pony house for over twenty years.

Angie walked back into the kitchen and opened a cabinet. She pulled out a bottle of Irish Mist. She poured a shot, turned toward Maeve's bedroom door and held up her glass.

"To you, Mamma," she said aloud. "You did right by me."

Angie downed the shot in one swallow. "Now, I swear, I'll do right by you."

Angie put down the glass, took one last look at her sleeping dog and headed back into the cold, wet night.

Chapter Sixteen
The Phone Call to Action

Elsbeth Novak picked up the phone from the heavily carved pine desk, walked to the soft leather recliner and heaved a sigh as she lowered herself into its buttery smoothness. The den was James W.'s room to be sure, its heavy paneling and assortment of antique weaponry a tribute to his masculinity. He'd made sure of it when they'd built the five-bedroom ranch fifteen years ago. "You can have every other room in the house, Elsbeth," he'd said. "This one is mine."

Well, tonight James W. was on duty, and Elsbeth wanted to be comfortable for her phone call with Jimmy Jr. Sure enough, the call came in at precisely ten o'clock.

"Sheriff Novak's residence," she answered officiously. She loved the fact that her husband had a title of such import. Add to that she had started out a Wilks—third cousin on the father's side—and she'd married a Wilks. Well, technically James W. was a Novak, but he was half-Wilks, anyway. That meant she remained a member of the famous Wilks Dynasty for which the town and county were named. Elsbeth figured she had plenty to be proud of.

As Elsbeth Novak saw it, she was the most important woman living in Wilks, Texas, now. Miss Olivia—well, Miss Olivia was old.

"Hi, Mom. It's me."

Elsbeth smiled. "Jimmy." She settled back into the chair. The leather squeaked beneath her weight. "How's your day been?"

"Long."

Elsbeth heard the weariness in her son's voice and her heavy brow wrinkled. "Are you all right?"

"Tired," came the reply, and Elsbeth could picture her fit son pulling off his tie and sitting on the edge of the bed in some hotel room. "I'm in the Panhandle tonight," he said, answering her unasked question. "Never shook so many hands or ate so much barbecue in my life."

"You make sure you wash your hands," Elsbeth said.

She heard a chuckle on the other end but let it pass.

"I heard Maeve O'Day was murdered," Jimmy said, by way of conversation.

Elsbeth sat up with a start, and the chair's footrest went down with a thud. "It was an accident," she said tersely.

"That's not what Henry Jacobs said."

"When did you talk with Henry?"

"He called Leroy, my press agent. Thought he'd catch me up on the news."

"He shouldn't be botherin' you with such gossip."

"Mom, that's all we did as roommates through four years at UT. Besides, why would anybody want to kill a nice old lady like Maeve O'Day?"

Elsbeth stood, her face turning purple. "Nobody killed her, and how can you call a woman of that reputation nice? She was a dark smear on this town."

"Mom, Maeve O'Day was harmless."

"Is that all we're goin' to talk about tonight?" She huffed.

"I'm looking forward to coming home," he said hopefully. "Thinking maybe your sauerbraten might be the best thing to perk up a tired candidate."

Elsbeth's mood brightened. "You'll be home for supper on Saturday?"

"If everything goes all right. I'll call Friday night to confirm. After the Kiwanis fund-raiser in Midland."

"You're not callin' me for two nights?"

"Mom, I won't be home until after midnight the next few nights. There's a lot of hands to shake between now and November."

"I suppose so," she said. She would pay the price to have her son in the governor's mansion, but she didn't have to like it.

"On this Maeve O'Day thing, though, Mom. Since I'm coming in to speak on Sunday, isn't this something I could use to talk about my crime message? I mean, little old ladies aren't safe anymore. That kind of thing? Leroy thinks we could get some mileage out of it."

"James Wilks Novak Jr., I won't hear you preach about that woman from the pulpit on Sunday. Your grandmother would keel over right there in the pew."

"If you say," he hedged, "I won't talk about it from the pulpit. But I still think the outrage angle is a good one to play. Maybe I could hold a press conference after church or something."

Before Elsbeth could reply, Jimmy was getting off the phone. "Room service is here, Mom. Gotta get some real food. Hey, watch for me on KXAN. They had a camera crew at my luncheon speech today. They're giving me lots of air. Love you."

The phone clicked dead, and Elsbeth put it back in its brass-embossed cradle. She stared at it for a moment, then at the clock. She'd have to catch the midnight version of the Austin news.

She crossed to the green, marble-tiled entranceway, put on her suede coat, and walked out into the night.

Chapter Seventeen
An Unexpected Visitor

"Angie."

Matt Hayden let the word escape on an exhalation of surprise as he opened the parsonage's front door.

"I know it's late, Preacher. But you said anytime." A crack of thunder rent the air behind her, and Angie jumped. "I'm a little antsy, I guess."

She was standing there, dripping from the hard rain that framed her silhouette against the street light. She glistened with the life of the storm; the lightning reflected in her eyes. Wildness glowed in her cheeks.

Matt shook his head. Noticing things like that was not the way to start a conversation with Angie O'Day.

"Not too late at all," he said and opened the door wider for her to enter.

The parsonage was an average-sized affair, its walls painted antique white for whoever might be the occupant du jour. Matt's small furniture collection—a secondhand couch and a brown La-Z-Boy rocker—sat in front of the brown-brick fireplace. Unpacked boxes littered the room. The only light in the room came from the corner where a halogen scoop illuminated the ceiling.

Matt looked with disgust at the framed pictures that leaned against the far wall. He hadn't taken the time to hang them yet. He'd done little to personalize the place since he'd moved in seven weeks earlier.

"Homey," Angie said as she walked into the room.

Matt wanted to glare but resisted the urge. "You're soaking wet."

"Clouds burst right as I came across the bridge."

Matt looked out the window as the mantel clock struck ten o'clock. "Can't see across the street," he commented.

Angie walked over to the fireplace and checked the flue. "It's open." She pulled two logs from the bin that had been full since before Matt had moved in, then fished a lighter out of her pocket. She looked up at him after the first dry bark caught. "What? I'm cold."

"Can I get you some coffee?" The tug of appreciation he felt at the wet clothes hugging her body had him walking away. Fast. "A towel, maybe?"

Angie didn't notice his discomfort. "Coffee. I guess you don't have anything stronger?"

"I might be able to find a glass of wine."

"Make it two. I don't like to drink alone."

He went into the kitchen and emerged moments later with two paper cups filled with a Merlot. "I don't do dishes." His smile was sheepish. "But the laundry is a must." He handed her a terry towel.

"The life of a bachelor," Angie replied. She took the cup he offered, then sat on the edge of the couch. "I guess you're wonderin' why I'm here."

Actually he could care less why she was there. He was fascinated with watching her rub the towel over her hair and shoulders. He brought himself back to the conversation with effort.

"I'm figuring it has to do with your mother." He sat in the recliner.

She chuckled. "Not a hard figure." She sipped her wine, grimaced, then put it down on the crate of books before her. "Might as well get to it. Do you still think Mamma was murdered?"

Matt sighed. He'd been expecting her inquiry—only not at ten o'clock at night.

He took a sip of his own wine, then realized with dismay it had turned to vinegar. So much for offering her a drink, he thought. He put his cup down on a box.

"My brother was a cop," he said flatly. "You might say it was the family business."

Angie recognized the reply for what it was. She'd tended bar too often not to know when a man had a story to tell. The relationship between a bartender and her patron was about as sacred as a preacher and his parishioner, she figured. She nodded for him to continue.

"Five years ago my brother, Bry . . . sorry, Bryson . . . was working a drug bust in . . . another state." Careful, boy, he told himself. Witness protection programs were not about giving out details, yet he had to make Angie understand where he was coming from. "He had Crutches with him." He smiled at her puzzlement. "Crutches was his dog. Canine cop."

Matt leaned back in his chair. "Crutches and Bry had worked together for six years. Bry trained him. He lived with us."

"A member of your family," Angie murmured. "Like Shadow."

Matt nodded. "Crutches and my brother were responsible for bringing in over two million dollars' worth of illegal substances."

"They were a good team."

"Until a warehouse raid they were doing right before Christmas. When Crutches set off a bomb that was hidden in a suspicious shipment. He and Bry blew two hundred feet into the air."

Angie furrowed her brow. "Drugs and explosives? That doesn't sound like two things a trained police dog would mix up."

"Crutches was trained to sniff drugs, not explosives. The bomb was hidden in a stash of crack. Explosives-trained dogs sit. Drug dogs go after the packages like they sniffed their first meal in weeks."

"That made it obvious the bomb was a plant, right?"

"Not to the Miami Chief of Police. Howard P. Rutledge, believed otherwise."

Great. Now he'd let the perp's name slip. What was he doing?

"So, someone put crack in with the explosives—" Angie looked horrified. "—To get your dog to trigger a bomb? That's awful."

Matt took a drink of his wine, despite its sour taste. He'd better not go any farther down this road. His Federal Marshall would have a cow if he knew Matt had spilled this much information. *"First your dad, then your brother. You wanna be next?"*

"How did you stand it?"

Matt shook off the memory. "I didn't. My brother and that dog were murdered." Matt looked at her. "I don't know how else to say it. I hated."

"How do you live with knowin' he was murdered and no one would do anything about it?"

Matt stared into the flames. "I don't. I give that part to God to handle."

"That's why you became a pastor."

"I had the choice of hating day in and day out, letting that hate consume me, or of loving day in and day out. Letting that love consume me."

Angie sneered. "That's a cop-out."

"Nope," Matt said quietly. "That's a solution. Mine, anyway." He got to his feet.

"How did your mom, your family, feel about that solution?"

Matt closed his eyes and drew a breath. "Let's just say we don't talk much anymore." He snorted. "My fiancé opted out.

She was prepared to be a cop's wife. Not a minister's wife." He still remembered the day she turned down going into the witness protection program with him. It was as if someone had turned a knife in his heart.

Angie's eyes rounded in surprise. "You were engaged."

"I can be lovable," he said easily. Too easily, he realized.

She studied his face. Though he was smiling now, he was hiding something. Something important. Maybe he was right, though. The more she learned about this man of the cloth, the more she was beginning to like him.

She lightened the topic. "So you were goin' to be a cop?"

"I was going to be a darned good cop," he said, sensing a challenge. "Why?"

"You don't seem like the cop type," she said.

"I did then."

A crash of thunder sounded overhead. Matt got up and walked to the fireplace. "Might lose the power at this rate," he said, shifting the logs.

"I'd better get home." Angie put her wine on the box, stood and headed for the door. "I've got my answer, Preacher. Now I have to decide what to do with it."

"I don't feel I've been much help."

Angie turned to him and let a hint of a smile tweak the corner of her mouth. She realized it was the first smile she'd felt in days. "You don't always have to play the preacher, you know."

He was ruffled. When Angie O'Day looked at him like that—her eyes half-smiling, half-knowing—his insides felt quite a jolt. "I'll get you a coat," he said, averting his gaze.

Matt reached past her to the entryway closet to get his to loan her. His hand grazed her shoulder and he dropped the slicker. Even more flustered, he stooped to pick it up but stopped cold when she put her hand on his shoulder.

Angie grinned. "Have you been around women much since you've become a pastor?"

Matt swallowed uncomfortably, straightened and held the coat up for her to take.

"Well, don't worry, Preacher. When I make a move on you, it won't be because I feel sorry for you, or 'cuz you caught me at a bad time." She shrugged into the coat.

"I'm sorry," Matt said.

All pretense of a smile dropped from her face. "You don't have anything to be sorry for."

"I've given you the wrong impression."

"You haven't given me a wrong impression. You're as interested in me as I am in you. The difference between us is that you'd feel it was a sin if you did kiss me, and I wouldn't." She squared her shoulders. "I don't bring men to sin." She pulled open the front door, and a slap of rain hit them both hard. "Even preachers." With that, she turned and walked out into the night.

***

Miss Olivia clutched her fist to her heart. The pain was happening again. Just as it had thirty-five years ago. Was it a simple physical reaction to the emotional stress she'd been enduring, or maybe punishment for deeds better left to a higher power?

God had given her the strength to be married to Cash Novak. Surely, he would give her five more minutes to crawl to the phone and call for help.

The pain streaked down her arm, her left arm. She knew the signs all too well. She could barely catch her breath as she pulled herself across the hallway to the phone that rested on the antique table by the front door.

The phone and marble table crashed to the floor. She pulled the receiver to her ear. Her breath was so heavy in her chest, she couldn't suck in enough fresh air to push out the old.

More from rote than from thought, she dialed the familiar phone number of her beloved son.

James W. Everything had always been for James W. And now, Jimmy, Jr. The Wilks name would live on in honor.

The last thing Miss Olivia remembered was a ringing sound in her ears. Whether it was from the phone or her own dizziness, she'd never be certain.

Chapter Eighteen
Roth and Cash

Having lent his raincoat to Angie, Matt Hayden was dripping wet when he entered the waiting room of the Wilks Medical Clinic.

"I appreciate your gettin' here so quick." Sheriff James W. Novak stubbed out his cigarette and rose from an uncomfortable-looking chair.

Matt shook the rain off his umbrella before easing the door closed behind him. The rain was turning to ice. The umbrella had done little to protect him against the windblown sleet, but the two-block brisk walk from the parsonage had gone a long way to clearing Matt's head of Angie's visit.

"How is Miss Olivia?" Matt asked after solemnly shaking the sheriff's hand.

"Dicey." James W. locked his thumbs in his uniform belt loops. "Guess we've been lucky so far. She hasn't had a real attack for a long time now." He looked fearfully at the solid steel door that separated the waiting room from the clinic's

127

emergency room. "They're tryin' to stabilize her."

"Heart attack, then?"

"Yep. We're lucky she made it to the phone. Elsbeth got the call. She didn't hear anything but breathin'. Thank God she didn't think it was a pervert on the other end of the line."

Matt nodded and suppressed a smirk.

James W. eyed the pastor carefully. "I know Elsbeth has given you some grief over the last few days, Preacher, but she's really a good heart."

"Of course she is, Sheriff," Matt said earnestly. "I apologize if I've intimated otherwise."

"You didn't." James W.'s smile was sheepish. "I just know my wife, that's all."

Matt did his best not to smile back and decided it would be diplomatic to change the subject. He spied a coffee bar in the corner. The coffee steamed with a rich roasted scent. "Fresh coffee," he said appreciatively.

"Just finished brewing." James W. sat down hard on the couch.

Matt poured himself a cup, then reached for the sugar. He'd learned way back that pastors spent long nights in hospital waiting rooms.

"You know, that's what attracted me to Elsbeth," James W. said.

"Excuse me?" Matt asked. He took the chair catty-corner from the sheriff.

"Elsbeth. I know she has a mouth on her, but that's one of the things that attracted me to her." James W. shook his head.

"My mother, she's always so close-mouthed. Never says much of anything, good or bad. You have to guess with her." He let out a chuckle. "You never have to guess with Elsbeth. She tells you what's on her mind, no matter what it is. It was kind of refreshing not to have to guess where I stood all the time."

"I was over to your mamma's house today. Beautiful mansion."

"Mamma wasn't too happy when Elsbeth and me built the place outside of town. That mansion's been in the Wilks family for over a hundred and fifty years."

"Elsbeth didn't want to live in the mansion?" Matt sipped his coffee.

James W. laughed. "She wants the Wilks mansion, all right, but not with Mamma in it. They're two strong-willed women, Pastor." He cast a glance toward the parking lot door. "Elsbeth'll be here shortly. She's callin' Jimmy Jr. to tell him about Miss Olivia." He picked up the Styrofoam coffee cup from the stained wood end table and downed it in one gulp. "Yeah, Elsbeth and Miss Olivia might be a different pattern, but they're sure cut from the same cloth."

"Your mother has always been the quiet type?" Matt searched for conversation. He hadn't found that to be exactly true. Miss Olivia had definitely had her say at coffee earlier. The sheriff wanted to talk, however, and Matt was there to comfort.

"Mamma believes that a closed mouth catches no flies. That's probably one reason she has heart trouble. Keeps everything inside." Too restless to sit, James W. got to his feet and began pacing. "My mother has seen a lot of trouble in her life. More than her share."

"Your brother was killed in Iran, I understand?"

"Helluva time, that. Carter sent Operation Eagle Claw, that's what they called it, to free the hostages. After 'Nam, we'd let our secret ops go down the tubes. Didn't need them, said the Washington bean counters. But then the Shah came to the U.S. to get his teeth filled or some such bullshit, and the U.S. was welcomed into the world of international terrorism. Roth volunteered to go into the Special Forces Group that was supposed to rescue the hostages. He was one of three marines who died. The Navy lost five."

He turned and looked at the pastor. "Miss Olivia and Cash had their problems, but both of them sure were proud of that boy."

"Problems?"

"Well, Roth was my half-brother, actually. Cash Novak was a widower when he married Miss Olivia."

"I didn't know."

"It was a long time ago. Miss Olivia was the last of the Wilks. Cash . . . well . . . my pa was a scoundrel. There's no doubt about that. The only person he ever really cared for was his first wife, Geneva Yeck. Warren and Ben's youngest sister. When she died . . . well, he didn't care about much anymore."

"He married Miss Olivia, didn't he?"

"That was pretty much the decision of the two families. Miss Olivia was an only child—the last of the Wilks. She was four foot eight, not what you might call pretty . . . well." He shrugged. "She was headin' into spinsterhood real quick. And Cash was so distraught over Geneva's passin' he wasn't much of a father. So the two most prominent families in town, the Novaks and the Wilks, decided Cash and Miss Olivia should get married. Then all the money and Roth's care would be wrapped up in one nice package."

"Cash and Miss Olivia's marriage was arranged."

"Times were different back then, Preacher. Good people didn't take hand-outs. Roth needed to be cared for. The Wilks wanted their line continued. A person did what had to be done. Miss Olivia, she did her duty."

"Duty," Matt repeated. Something in Matt snapped. "She had you."

James W. smiled. "And made sure the Wilks line would go strong for another generation." He sat back down on the couch. "It was enough for her to have a son with Wilks blood, even if she had a marriage with no love. That's why I'm not a Junior after my pa. She made sure my middle name is Wilks, so that I'd never forget my blood."

"More coffee?" Matt asked, getting to his feet.

"I'm Lutheran, ain't I?" James W. grinned and held out his cup. "Can't blame her much," he said, more to himself than Matt. "Cash Novak was a rounder."

Matt poured two fresh cups of coffee and brought one back to the sheriff. "Cash died not too long after Roth, right?"

"First Roth. Then Pa. That's when Miss Olivia had her first heart attack. Broken heart, I always said."

"Now here we are, thirty-five years later."

"Same waitin' room." James W. looked around. "Same awful fake leather couches. Heck, even the same plastic plants. Some things don't change, I guess."

The cell phone on James W.'s wide black leather belt went off. He checked the number. "It's Elsbeth," he said, and brought it to his ear. "Hi, hon."

The sheriff's face paled. He listened some more, mumbled an expletive, then finished with, "I'll be right there." He snapped the phone back onto his belt.

"Problem?" Matt asked.

"Elsbeth's on her way over. Could you stay until she gets here?" James W. picked up his coffee cup, poured its contents into the plastic palm tree, and tossed it in the trashcan. "Then come on over to Ernie's Sinclair Station. Pearl's gonna need you." James W. grabbed up his khaki jacket and threw it over his shoulders. "Call me if Mamma's condition changes."

Matt stood. "What's going on?"

The sheriff slapped his hat on his head. His mouth was set in a hard line. "Ernie didn't come home for dinner, so Pearl went lookin' for him. Found him on the floor of the garage. Dead."

Chapter Nineteen
This Is Murder

"What do you figure happened?" Matt squatted by the body of Ernie Masterson. A neat white chalk mark was drawn around the outline of the body. That was the nicest thing he could say about the scene before him.

Ernie lay at the back bumper of Grace Lutheran's Aerostar van parked in the middle bay of the Sinclair Station. His face was crushed in on one side as if he had hit a wall. On the other side of his head, a small dent was caved into his skull. A can of Dr. Pepper was spilled on the floor beneath him.

Despite the fact the garage door was now open, the fumes of car exhaust were heavy in the air.

"I think someone wants us to think this was either an accident or a suicide," James W. said. He had the door of the van open and was studying the dashboard.

"It isn't," Matt agreed flatly.

The deputy, James W.'s only other official on the scene, looked up from where he photographed Ernie's body. "How can you be so sure? Ernie turned on the motor to do himself in, then slipped on the soda as he came around the truck."

"Richard Dube, how long you been workin' for me?" James W. stuck his head out the Ford's cab.

Richard cleared his skinny throat, which separated his skinny head from his skinny body. "Three weeks."

"Now, your daddy was a good sheriff. Mainly 'cuz Danny Don knew when to listen and when to shut up. This is your time to shut up."

The deputy's pock-ridden face reddened.

"Dube," Pastor Hayden repeated. "You're Sheriff Danny Don Dube's son?"

"Yes, sir." Mortified, Richard Dube returned to his job of taking pictures of the dead Ernie Masterson.

"Well, don't be feelin' too bad, son," Matt said kindly. "Someone went to a lot of work to make this look like a suicide. It doesn't figure, that's all."

"What don't figure?"

"That somebody who wants to kill himself starts the motor of a truck, but opens himself a Dr. Pepper before he starts suckin' fumes." James W. climbed down from the cab and slammed the door shut. "Get a good shot of his hands. They're as greasy as ever."

Matt looked up questioningly at the sheriff. "No smears on the ignition or keys," James W. explained.

"So we had us an accident on Friday and a murder on Tuesday," Matt said.

James W. moved over to the pegboard by the empty first

bay where all of Ernie's tools hung.

They were in order, Matt realized with surprise. Ernie had never struck him as the organized type.

"I know what you're thinkin', Pastor. You still think Maeve O'Day's death was more than an accident." James W. stepped closer to the tools, studying them intently. "I can't justify hanging murder on some fool for shooting a lost old woman with Alzheimer's who was in the wrong place at the wrong time." He motioned to the deputy with his hand, still looking at the wall. "Richard, come 'ere."

Obediently, Richard Dube took a last picture of Ernie's grease-encrusted hands, then went to the sheriff.

"Right here, Richard." James W. pointed at the row of crowbars.

All but one hung with the looped end facing the office door.

Richard snapped off three or four pictures and in the last one, James W. pointed to the crowbar with the loop pointed away from the office door. His hand still gloved, he pulled down the crowbar that hung in the opposite position. He walked over to Ernie's body and held the curve of the crowbar above the curve of the small indent in Ernie's skull.

Even from where Matt stood, he could see that the arc of the crowbar mirrored the impression flattened into Ernie's skull.

James W. looked at Richard, then at Matt. "But this," he said pointedly, "is murder."

Chapter Twenty
The Night the Lights Went Out

Pearl Masterson lived simply, but she struck Matt as being the type that didn't demand much from life to begin with. The apartment above the Sinclair Station had been the home of Pearl and Ernie Masterson since the day they were married. Olive shag carpeting, a holdover from the seventies Matt imagined, ran throughout the quaint two-bedroom home. In the kitchen, where Matt sat holding Pearl's hand, navy blue and white checks dominated the decor, with an occasional slice of watermelon on a towel here, a cornice there.

The four of them, Matt, James W., Richard Dube, and Pearl, were gathered in the small kitchen. Matt decided Pearl found comfort in staying busy. The sound of a washer and dryer running came from the adjoining mudroom. The scent of fresh coffee filled the air. Apricot kolaches steamed on the small kitchen table. Now, with her busy work finished, Pearl allowed herself to sit.

She'd already been crying, Matt noted. Her eyes were puffy,

her nose swollen. What little bottom lip she had, she'd worried red.

"It looked like he slipped," Pearl said quietly. James W. shifted his weight against the counter and stared out the window above the sink into the black night. "It looked that way, Pearl. That don't mean it happened that way."

"Was he . . ." She took a deep breath. "Drunk?"

"We'll have to wait for the autopsy," James W. said.

Pearl sighed at the word and closed her eyes.

"I'm sorry, Pearl, but I've got to know what Ernie's movements were tonight." James W.'s voice was gentle, and Matt could see the interview was hard for him. Pearl was as close to a sister as James W. had. "Richard's gonna write down what you say, all right?"

Dutifully, Richard Dube pulled out a notepad and pen from his jacket and hunched down over the table to write.

"He didn't come home," Pearl said. "I called over to the garage when it got late. He didn't answer. I figured he'd gone drinkin'." She took a shaky sip from her coffee.

"He did that a lot," James W. prodded.

"More and more lately," she said. "Then Elsbeth called." She leaned forward in her chair. "I'm sorry, James W. You need to be at the hospital."

"Elsbeth is with Miss Olivia. This is where I need to be."

"I went downstairs to the garage. On the off-chance that he was there." She let out a sigh. "Then I was gonna head to the Ice House."

"But you didn't have to."

"No. The van's motor was running. I heard it before I went in." Pearl gave a snort. "I felt relieved. Thought it meant Ernie was working."

"What door did you go in?"

"The office." She sipped her coffee. "Like always."

"Was the door open?"

She nodded. "Unlocked."

"Any sign of struggle?"

"No." Pearl put down her cup and stared at it for a long moment. "Was it suicide, James W.? The motor running?"

"Did Ernie act like a man who wanted to take his life?" James W. asked.

Pearl considered for a moment and shook her head. "Can't imagine that."

"What has his mood been lately?" James W. came up to the table and pulled out the chair beside Matt. "Was he upset about Maeve O'Day bein' killed on his property?"

"Upset? Mad, more like." Pearl poured James W. a cup of coffee as he sat down. "Yesterday. At that Yankee." She offered cream, knowing James W. would accept it.

Matt struggled not to ask some questions of his own, but the sheriff had already told him in this situation a preacher's job was to listen. Period.

"Anything different about today?" James W. prompted.

"It was normal." The dryer tone sounded and Pearl pushed away from the table. She walked toward the laundry room. "For Ernie."

"What does that mean, Pearl?" James W. asked.

"You know Ernie, James W." Restlessly she opened the dryer door and hauled the load onto its top. She began folding the jeans and hanging work shirts. Matt nodded. In his experience, everyday routine sometimes offered the best solace to those who were in shock.

"He started out with a hangover," James W. said.

Pearl continued to fold a T-shirt, but she nodded.

"What time did he get home last night?" This question came from Matt, and he immediately felt the sheriff's disapproval.

"Midnight or so," Pearl said. Her eyes lit with interest and she turned toward Matt. "Had some interesting things to say about you and that O'Day woman."

Matt grimaced. "I'll bet he did."

"I'm glad you were there for Angie," Pearl said, a tinge of independence pushing into her tone. "That girl's been through enough." She went back to folding but stopped as she picked up an item and stood stock-still.

"Got a problem with your laundry there, Pearl?" James W. pushed away from the table and walked to the mudroom.

"No, no problem," she mumbled, but James W. held her elbow as she went to return the load to the dryer.

"What's this?" he asked as he reached over and pulled a cloth from her hand.

Pearl swallowed. "I'm always washing rags from the station."

"This ain't no rag." James W. held it up for Matt to see. "This here's a bandanna."

A black bandanna, Matt realized.

"Where'd this come from?" James W. pushed on.

"Really, James W., I don't know when I picked that up." Pearl tossed the remainder of the laundry in the dryer and slapped the door shut.

"Mind if I keep this, Pearl?" James W. asked, and handed it to Richard Dube. "What made you go over to the station tonight?" James W. changed his line of questioning. "He's out late most nights."

"Elsbeth called looking for him. Right as the ten o'clock news started, I guess." Pearl returned to the table and sat down. "The storm was real bad. Her cell phone was breaking up something fierce. I got to worryin' where he might be."

"Was there any money missin' from the cash register at the station tonight?"

Pearl, her hands shaking, poured herself another cup of coffee. "Elsbeth told me to check that first off when I called her back, looking for you. As far as I could tell, it was all there. I left work at four this afternoon. Had to run to the grocer's before making supper."

"Was Ernie alone when you left the garage?" James W. continued.

"Tom Gibbons was working."

"Who?" Matt asked.

"High school kid. Been working with Ernie for a coupla years now. Tryin' to learn how to be a mechanic," James W. explained.

Matt had a hard time picturing Ernie Masterson as a mentor for some high school kid.

"Comes in after school, works through eight. Does cash

register for the supper crowd. You know, people heading home from work," Pearl addressed this again to Matt. "He might've been the last one to see. . ." Her eyes clouded over, and she laid her head in her hand.

"That's enough for now, Pearl. Who can I get to stay with you?" James W. said.

"Elsbeth—" she started to say. "But not with Miss Olivia sick." She lifted her head and looked around the room as if someone else would appear.

"I can stay here with you," Matt volunteered.

Her eyes focused on the laundry room for a long moment. "I'll call somebody," she said quietly. "You need to be with Miss Olivia."

Richard Dube closed his notebook and James W. headed for the back door. "You've got my cell number, Pearl. Use it if you need me."

Matt stood and gave her hand one last squeeze. "I'll be at the hospital with Miss Olivia, Pearl."

"I appreciate it, Preacher," Pearl said. She stood. "What about arrangements?" Her voice dropped to a whisper. "For the funeral?"

"I'll call you first thing in the morning. After I hear from the coroner," James W. assured her.

Pearl nodded. She saw the men to the door and closed it behind them.

"Maybe I shouldn't leave her alone," Matt wondered aloud when the three men got outside. His breath froze in the frigid air.

"My guess is she won't be alone for long. There're a lot of folks in this town that care for that woman," James W. answered. He turned to his deputy. "Richard, stay here and set up surveillance on the Sinclair Station."

Richard shuddered in his jacket, but said, "Yes, sir."

"I'll be at the hospital. Keep a sharp eye."

"For what?"

"If anyone comes over. Write down their names."

Richard nodded, then peeled off to the alley beside the garage.

"You know who wears black bandannas, don't you?" James W. asked quietly.

"Yeah," Matt replied. Every employee at the Fire and Ice House was wearing black bandannas in mourning for Maeve O'Day. Pearl Masterson had been laundering a black bandanna, and she'd been obvious in trying to hide it from James W. Matt shook his head. That made things look a little more than suspicious.

Suddenly a spark flew down from overhead. Matt and James W. ducked, then looked up to see what had happened.

A tree branch, heavy with ice from the earlier storm, leaned heavily on the wires that stretched between Ernie's Sinclair Station and the Fire and Ice House.

"It's gonna go!" the sheriff hollered as he shoved Matt back.

Sure enough, the limb cracked under the weight of the ice. It split from the trunk and fell to the ground, taking both the power lines with it.

Another spark, followed by a bead of fire, trailed up the lines to the transformer attached to the pole twenty feet ahead of them. Both men jumped at the sound of explosion as the transformer blew.

The lights in the surrounding houses flickered and then went out.

"That's the power," James W. said and spat on the ground.

Matt turned his head abruptly toward the Wilks Medical Clinic.

"They've got a generator, Preacher," James W. said. "These small electrical co-ops are worthless. We're used to dealin' with power outages." He looked toward the clinic. "Elsbeth ain't gonna like this one bit."

"You've got paperwork, I imagine," Matt said. "And utility companies to contact. I'll stay with Elsbeth and your mother."

James W. nodded, extended his hand. "I'm obliged to you, Preacher." He started toward the police station, then stopped. "About what I said in the truck on Sunday . . ."

Matt smiled. "It's forgotten."

Chapter Twenty-One
Tom Gibbons

"Mrs. Masterson told us you were working last night." James W.'s voice was tired as he questioned the teenager who helped out at Ernie's Sinclair Station after school.

Sheriff James W. had gotten little sleep the night before, but at least he'd had the chance to shower and change clothes. That was a sight better than Matt had fared. He'd spent the night with Elsbeth in the waiting room at the Wilks Medical Clinic. His gray slacks were wrinkled. His blue shirt was stained with coffee. Elsbeth, now allowed to sit in Miss Olivia's room, had looked as tired as he felt.

Much to Matt's chagrin, her voice was raw from a night of talking.

Miss Olivia's heart was still too unsteady and the roads too icy for an ambulance to take her to higher care. The doctor had called a consultation with the family after his morning rounds. The consultation that James W. and Matt were now awaiting.

Torn between his duty to his mother and his duty to his

office, James W. had asked Richard Dube to pick up Tom Gibbons, the high school employee at Ernie's Sinclair Station, and bring him to the hospital for an early morning interview.

The power might still be out in the town, but at least the hospital's small generator was spitting out warmth.

Matt noted the kid's pale hands were shaking, and his voice was thin. He wasn't used to talking to the police.

"What time did you leave work?" James W. asked.

"Eight." Tom Gibbons pulled his Pennzoil baseball cap lower on his brow, thus concealing the last bit of dark brown hair that had peeked out.

"Anything about Ernie make you think he was nervous about somethin'?"

"No." Tom studied the waiting room's linoleum floor, enticing Matt to do the same. Gray with pink, black, and white flecks. Blood would probably blend in pretty well on an as-needed basis with the medical center's floor.

"Ernie do anything out of the ordinary?" James W. asked.

"No."

James W. ran a tired hand over his face and Matt concealed a smile. The teenager had an instinctual fear of the police. James W. was going to get nowhere with this boy, and James W. knew Matt knew it.

"Preacher, can I have a word?" James W. asked, rising from the green-covered couch.

Matt nodded, and the two went over to the coffee pot in the corner. Matt shook off the sheriff's offer for a cup with a shudder. He'd drunk enough coffee in the last twenty-four hours to wire most of Austin.

"The kid's not gonna talk to me." James W. sighed.

"You're right." This time Matt did smile.

"Help me out here, will ya?" James W. was exhausted, and Matt felt immediately contrite. The man's mother had suffered a life-threatening heart attack, and his friend who might as well have been a member of his family had been murdered.

"Good cop, bad cop?" Matt offered.

James W. looked up in surprise, then nodded. "Guess it figures you're the good cop."

The two men turned back to the five-foot-six-inch youth. Tom was in the middle of a growth spurt. His raveled jeans were short, revealing grease-smeared Reeboks. Tom's jeans had the classic worn hole at the knee that seemed the style of every kid in Wilks. Matt wondered if the teenagers cut the holes in the cloth themselves or if they bought them that way.

"Tom, I'm Pastor Hayden," Matt said, sitting beside the youth.

Tom scooted over without looking up.

"You're an important person here, because you may have been the last one to see Ernie alive. Now, we know you didn't have anything to do with Ernie's dying, but you might have seen something that would help us figure out who did."

"I didn't see nothin'."

Matt mustered some encouragement that he'd managed to get more than one word out of the boy. "Let us figure that out. Now, what's a typical night of work for you at the Sinclair Station?"

Tom looked up, and Matt saw he had green eyes and pale skin—so pale the blue of the veins showed through on his eyelids and down his neck. It made Matt wonder the last time the kid had seen a fruit or vegetable on his dinner plate. "What do you do at work?"

"I tend the cash register. We're self-serve. Sometimes Ernie lets me watch him work on cars, so's I can learn, but from four to eight we're pretty busy."

"So you pretty much talk to everyone who comes to get gas."

"They've gotta pay me, don't they?" Tom said with a sniff.

"Ernie worked in the garage the whole time you were there?" This the sheriff interjected.

"Yeah." Tom reverted to the one-word answer.

"So you came in to work at four," Matt prodded.

"That's my time. You don't show up late to work at Ernie's."

"He'd let you know his displeasure?" James W. asked.

"He'd yell pretty bad," Tom agreed.

"Mrs. Masterson was running the cash register until you came." Matt stuck with what he knew.

Tom nodded.

Matt gave him an encouraging smile. "Who all came in and bought gas last night, Tom?"

"Most everybody in Wilks," Tom said with a shrug. "It was swamped. Everybody was tankin' up before that ice storm."

"Did anyone go in and talk to Ernie during your shift last night?"

"No . . ."

Matt and James W. looked at each other. There was

something there. Tom's answer was less assured. "Did Ernie come out and talk to anyone?"

Tom squirmed in his seat. "Not durin' my shift," he said finally.

"I guess you know you'd be in big trouble for holdin' somethin' back, Tom." James W. said, hauling both hands to rest authoritatively on his belt.

Tom nodded, but kept his mouth firmly closed.

"You'd be impedin' an official investigation. If you're hidin' any evidence, you might even be considered an accessory to a crime."

Tom swallowed audibly but kept his head down. James W. looked at Matt and nodded.

"Now, Sheriff, you can see this boy isn't a criminal. He just doesn't want to be a snitch."

Tom looked up hopefully at Matt, and Matt could see plainly that he was on the right tack.

"I'm the only one in my family workin' right now," Tom blurted out.

"Ernie's dead, son," James W. said quietly. "He can't fire you."

"Is that what you're frightened of, Tom? Getting fired?" Matt pressed.

Tom puffed out his chin, and Matt saw three strands of wiry black hair jutting from below his lip. He wondered if Tom had started shaving yet. "I ain't afraid of nothin'."

Matt decided then and there that Tom Gibbons was scared of just about everything.

"What time did you leave last night?" James W. continued.

"A little after eight. I locked the front door and came through the garage to tell Ernie I was leavin'."

"What was Ernie doing?"

"He was workin' on some old van. I said I was goin'. He said, 'Bye.' That was it."

Matt was trying to figure out how things worked. "So anyone who bought gas after you left had to go to the garage and pay Ernie."

"Yep. We don't have those fancy pay-at-the-pump things like they've got in Austin."

James W. shook his head. "I'll be talkin' to you more about this, Tom."

"Yessir." The youth jumped to his feet as he realized he'd been dismissed.

"Tell you what, Tom," Matt stood and pulled out his wallet. "If you think of anything else, give me a call." He handed over his card. "Why don't you head down to Callie Mae's Cafe and buy yourself a sandwich."

Tom looked eagerly at the ten-dollar bill that Matt handed him and nodded. "Thanks."

Matt and James W. watched him leave.

"What's he afraid of?" James W. wondered aloud. "Even if he saw Ernie doin' somethin' wrong, Tom couldn't get in trouble now."

"Maybe he's not afraid of Ernie." Matt sat back down.

"Who else, then?" James W. demanded.

"Perhaps the murderer."

James W. nodded. "You've got a point, Preacher." He looked at his watch. "Holy—" He jumped to his feet. "It's almost nine o'clock. I've got a peck of things I've got to be doin'. When's that doctor comin'?"

"Is there anything I can do to help?" Matt stood.

"I've gotta talk to the coroner, get the county records contacted." James W. shook his head. "It's all official business, Reverend, but I—" James W. paused. "Actually there is something that needs doing, but it's a little beneath your station."

"Name it, James W. I'll be happy to do whatever you need."

The sheriff looked sheepish, and Matt almost grinned. "Could you go over to the mansion and walk my mamma's dog?"

Chapter Twenty-Two
Take a Walk

Five minutes later, Matt Hayden crossed the square to Miss Olivia's mansion. *"Of course, I'll walk your Mamma's dog."* His breath puffed in the crisp air, and his smile was broad at the memory of James W.'s blush when the sheriff had made his request.

As instructed, Matt went around to the back of the Wilks mansion and entered through the kitchen. He still was amazed that folks in Wilks didn't lock their doors. He let Miss Olivia's Havanese out, then looked around. Since James W. was back at the clinic and no one else was anywhere to be seen, Matt allowed himself the privilege of a full-fledged belly laugh.

"Blanco, boy, you do your thing," he said cheerfully to the white dog, then followed the ball of long fur as it led the way down the red brick sidewalk.

This was the reason he'd spent three years in seminary, he chuckled. The reason he'd learned Greek and Hebrew, the reason he'd endured countless hours of lectures on homiletics and theology. The reason he'd forsaken a career in law enforcement so that he could be in the business of life enforcement.

All those choices, all those commitments, all so he could walk an elderly woman's long-haired, snowball-looking mass of fur on a freezing morning in the middle of a state where the people talked funny and the food bit your tongue before you could bite it.

At times like these, Matt truly believed the Almighty had a wicked sense of humor.

Blanco, having finished the necessities of life, headed back toward the mansion, and Matt followed cheerily along. He closed the kitchen door behind them, toweled off Blanco's tiny paws, then made sure the dog had fresh food and water.

The air in the house was chilly, and Matt decided to make sure the furnace was back on after last night's power outage. He searched the kitchen, then the hallway, walked through the dining room and finally found the thermostat located on the wall just outside the parlor. As he had suspected, the furnace had not come back on automatically when power returned.

Not wanting poor little Blanco to be too cold, Matt adjusted the furnace up to what he considered comfortable, then turned to leave out the front door.

The marble table that held the phone was still upended in the front hallway from when Miss Olivia had collapsed with her heart attack. Matt set it to rights. He picked up the phone, placed it on the table, then reached down and picked up Miss Olivia's gloves and scarf. They were still wet from the storm.

He looked around, found a closet tucked away beneath the main stairway, and opened the door. Everything was neatly ordered. Spring coat hung under plastic. Matching hat wrapped in plastic above it on the shelf. A light jacket hung to the side, a matching scarf around the hanger. Miss Olivia's heavy winter coat, brown wool with a nice fur collar, hung in the middle. He placed the leather gloves on the shelf right above the coat to dry, and he hung the scarf around the coat's hanger. He brought his hand away, wet. The fur collar from the coat was still damp from last night's storm as well. Well, with the furnace now on, everything should dry quickly.

Matt walked back into the kitchen, tossed a scrap from the cookie jar in Blanco's direction and then locked the door behind him.

Would that all his tasks as a minister were this easy. Something about the simple tasks of walking a dog and laying an old lady's scarf out to dry appealed to the servant in him he wanted to cultivate. Christ had called him to be a servant, a job that was easy to do when the tasks were definable. He let out a heavy sigh in the cold air and headed back toward the clinic. Now it was time to return to the not-so-easy side of servanthood.

The reality of murder.

***

"Here you go, Sheriff," Richard Dube said as he dumped all of the gas receipts from the Sinclair Station onto the hospital waiting room's round Formica table.

"What are we looking for, exactly?" Matt asked, plowing into the receipts. He guessed that there had to be at least thirty credit-card slips before him.

"Alphabetize 'em and write 'em all down. If Tom saw somethin', then chances are another customer might've seen somethin'," James W. said.

"These are only the credit sales. What about all of the cash transactions?" Matt asked.

"We'll start with these, and use 'em to get more names."

"Want me to help, James W.?" Richard Dube was eager to get in on the investigation.

James W. considered. "Naw. You'd best get back to the office and mind the phone. With all this ice, there's bound to be folks who need some help." Richard was disappointed, but he pulled his coat back on.

Heaving a sigh, James W. returned to the pile of receipts. "We'll begin with the ones that clocked in after Tom's shift started at four o'clock."

"Make it three o'clock," Matt suggested. "Tom said he didn't see anything on his shift. That suggests he might've seen something before or after."

James W. nodded. "Three until eight, then." He straddled the back of the plastic shell chair and grabbed up a fist full of receipts. "Let's get started."

Chapter Twenty-Three
Another Yeck History Lesson

"Warren, you in here?" Matt called into the dark tin shed behind Grace Lutheran's fellowship hall. Today was Thursday, Warren's usual day for cleaning the grounds before the busy church weekend. There was Two or One Club on Friday nights for the young couples and singles in the church, confirmation for the junior high kids on Saturday mornings, and, of course, services on Sunday.

Warren Yeck raised his head from behind a row of gas cans. He held a buzz saw in one hand and a can of gas in the other. "You want me, Pastor?" came the janitor's high-pitched reply.

"I've got James W. with me. We need to ask you a few questions," Matt called.

"Be right there," Warren said. He picked his way through the tool shed, mindful of the various implements and cans strewn along the way.

One thing Ernie Masterson had on Warren Yeck, Matt thought. Ernie kept a clean workshop.

The old man joined the sheriff and the pastor outside the shed. "Had some branches come down last night," Warren said, gazing up at an old tree. "Thought I'd better get 'em all cleared up before someone gets hurt."

"I appreciate it, Warren," the pastor said. Warren Yeck might not have been the neatest caretaker in the world, but he sure was a hard worker.

"Saw where you bought some gas at Ernie's Sinclair Station last night," James W. said, immediately getting down to business.

"Filled the tank," Warren agreed. "Television news cut in and said there was a bad ice storm headin' this way. I've got people up in Kerrville. It hit there first. I was talkin' to Emmy. That's my cousin from—"

"Fine, Warren," James W. said, cutting to the chase. Matt smiled. Warren would take all day to tell how he was related to the Kerrville Emmy if James W. let him. "What time did you pull into the station?"

Warren put down the gas can and thought for a moment. "Musta been around three-thirty. No, three-forty-five, I'd say. I'd turned off Andy Griffith. I really like that show. Always have. They run it every day on—"

"So it was after the Andy Griffith episode finished and time for you to get in your car and drive to the Sinclair."

"Yes, sir." Warren eyed the sheriff closely. Not many cut Warren Yeck off like that, but then again, not many were the sheriff of the town. "What's this all about?"

"When you went to the service station yesterday afternoon,

did you see or hear anything out of the ordinary?"

Warren peered even more closely at the sheriff, then put the saw down next to the gas can. "She's finally done it," he said with an approving nod.

"Who's done what?" James W. adjusted his hat against the morning sun rising over the church's roof.

"I've told her more than once to do somethin' about him."

Matt sent a questioning look James W.'s way, but the sheriff shrugged his puzzlement.

"Pearl finally filed a complaint against that man." Warren put his hands together as if saying a quick prayer of thanks to the Almighty. "'Bout time."

"What are you saying, Warren?" Matt asked.

"I know he's been a friend of your family's for a long time, James W.," Warren said. "It's probably what kept Pearl quiet all these years. If you ask me, it's been gettin' worse lately." The old man gestured toward a cement bench with Corinthian-style legs. "That's a start for an old man," he said, heading toward it. "Don't mind if I take a seat."

He lowered himself onto the bench, then studied the sheriff and the pastor. "So do you need me to be a witness, or what? I'll do it."

Matt started to speak, but James W. cut him off. "What exactly did you see at the gas station last night, Warren?"

"There's plenty folks about that say Pearl and that Bo fella over at the Fire and Ice House have a thing goin' on, but I don't believe it. Not one bit. But you can bet Ernie believed it."

"Bo. From the Fire and Ice House." James W. repeated.

"That's right. He was at the Sinclair buyin' gas—same as me. All he did was go inside and pay for it." Warren stood and faced Matt earnestly. "I'll swear to that on a stack of bibles, Reverend."

"What happened when he went inside?" Matt asked.

"Ernie came out of the garage and started throwin' a fit. Yelled at Bo—called him every name in the book. But Bo didn't say nothin' to him. Not one word. He just gave the money to Pearl and got back into his car."

"And that was it?" Matt asked.

"No, sir. That's when Ernie backhanded Pearl. A good one. Right across the mouth." Warren shook his head. "Bloodied her lip, he did. It ain't the first time either. Probably won't be the last."

"Actually, it might have been the last, Warren." James W. cleared his throat. "Ernie Masterson is dead."

Warren stared at the sheriff a long moment. "When did this happen? How?"

"During the ice storm last night," Matt said. "He was murdered."

"Now, wait a minute there." Warren stood. "You're not tryin' to say that Pearl had anything to do with murder, are you? There's plenty in this town that'll dance on that man's grave."

"Let's go inside and talk a bit, Warren. Get some hot coffee," James W. suggested.

Warren nodded. "Maybe we can find some good ole' Czech schnapps to toast the passing of that sonuva—" he looked at Matt and reconsidered, "—gun."

Chapter Twenty-Four
The Sheriff Visits the Ice House

"Bo, what are you doin' here so early?" Dorothy Jo Devereaux looked up from the celery she was chopping as Bo walked in the Fire and Ice House's kitchen door. He wore a navy plaid CPO jacket against the morning's freeze, Dorothy Jo noted with approval. That boy rarely took good enough care of himself.

"Angie called. Said we needed a meetin'." Bo leaned over her work area and picked up a celery stick. "To get here before the bar opened."

"That's for cooking." Dorothy Jo shook her head but returned to her work. "Land sakes, son, when do you sleep?"

"Got to bed at two. Never could sleep past seven." He chomped noisily on the celery and reached for another.

"You giving Bo a bad time, Dorothy Jo?" Angie entered through the kitchen's swinging doors. Shadow peeked into the kitchen, then went to his corner by the bar's wood stove. He wasn't allowed near the food preparation area.

"Person's got to get enough sleep," Dorothy Jo mumbled, never looking up from her celery. "What's this meetin' about, anyway?"

Angie walked over to the industrial-sized refrigerator and grabbed out a gallon of milk. She poured herself a cup. "I'm wonderin' if the two of you can handle things around here for a while. Alone."

That brought Dorothy Jo's head up with a snap. "Alone?"

Bo took the stool across from where Dorothy Jo worked. "Why?"

Angie drank the milk and rinsed out her cup. To Dorothy Jo it looked as if the simple act had exhausted the poor girl. "I need to do some thinkin'."

"Thinkin'," Dorothy Jo repeated. She put down her knife. "'What about, honey?"

"'Bout Mamma. What I need to do. Call it a vacation, I guess."

Dorothy Jo nodded. "Lord knows you deserve a vacation." The cook had been after her boss to take some kind of vacation for years.

"Where?" Bo asked.

"Corpus."

Bo looked out the window over the sink. "It's January," he commented. "Ain't much like beach weather."

"I'm not goin' there to swim." Angie smiled. "Just walk."

"And think," Dorothy Jo finished for her.

"It's gonna take a bit to get over your mamma's dyin'," Bo said.

"It's not just her dyin'." Angie's voice was quiet, but firm. "I knew that was comin'. It's a matter of deciding what I can live with and what I can't."

Dorothy Jo felt a twinge of dread. Angie looked so sad. "What're you talkin' about, honey?"

Angie studied her two friends closely. They were the only family she had left. "I was wonderin' . . ." She paused, knowing the question she was about to ask would shock them as much as it would exhaust her.

Dorothy Jo and Bo looked at her expectantly.

"I was wondering if the two of you would be interested in buying the Fire and Ice House?"

The words fell like mud pies on the floor, leaving a sticky mess between the three that Angie wasn't sure she could clean up.

"Buy it?" Bo echoed.

"What're you gonna do?" Dorothy Jo asked simultaneously.

"I don't have anything to keep me here in Wilks anymore." Except you two, she thought. She swallowed hard. "There's a lot of memories in this place. Bad ones. I think maybe it's time for me to move on."

"Where to?" Dorothy Jo demanded. "This is your home."

"Home is where I decide it is. I've lived thirty-five years with people here callin' me a whore or worse. That's not real homey, if you ask me."

"The whole town doesn't feel that way," Dorothy Jo argued. "Just those damned Wilks."

"Somebody took Mamma eight miles out of town and

dumped her on a deer lease so she could get shot."

That was the real issue. She could stand living in a town where people thought she was something she wasn't. She'd done that all of her life and snubbed her nose at them all. Heck, she'd even named her bowling team "The Hellraisers" so that the Lutheran Church would be forced to put a bad word in their bulletin every time the church team played hers. She'd learned later that Mrs. Fullenweider had shortened the name to "H-Raisers," but everyone knew what it stood for just the same.

She couldn't stand living in a town where someone had hated enough to kill her mamma. She wasn't sure she could live with that fact without becoming an animal herself.

Dorothy Jo was stunned. "You're really thinkin' of leaving town."

A gruff sound came from the direction of the swinging doors, and the three of them turned to find James W. standing in the doorway, Shadow wagging his tail traitorously at the sheriff's heel. James W. rested one hand on the doorjamb, the other on the weapon which hung at his belt.

"I wouldn't do that, Angie girl," he said, his voice deep and officious. "Not yet, anyway."

"What do you want, James W.?" Angie shook her head wearily. She was tired. Too tired for this.

"I'll talk to Bo first. Then you."

***

Sheriff James W. Novak kicked his boot up on the edge of the booth and looked hard into Bo's face. He had to find a murderer, however, and Bo had already killed once. James W. couldn't leave this stone unturned.

"I've got a problem I'm lookin' into, Bo, and I need your help."

"Horse manure, James W. You've got a murder and you need a suspect."

James W. put down his boot with a thud. "How do you know I've got a murder?"

Bo shrugged. He liked James W. The sheriff hadn't leaned on him once since he'd gotten to town. Bo figured those days of tolerance were over, though. "Word travels."

"Not for everybody," James W. said, thinking of Warren. "Somebody told you."

"Maybe." Bo studied the scarred surface of the table. He wondered if the sheriff knew the wood for the booths and tables was pilfered from the leftover pews when Grace renovated twenty-five years earlier.

"You worked right across the street from the Sinclair Station last night," James W. said reasonably. "I need to know if you saw anything. Heard anything."

"Did anything," Bo filled in for him.

"Did you do anything?" James W. turned the question.

"I pulled beers last night like always," Bo said. "Turned on the generator for the freezer and TV when the power went out. Got out the candles. Folks could still buy the beers that were on ice. Closed up at one a.m."

"So, other than the power going out, it was a normal night."

"Normal."

"Who were your customers?" James W. settled his weight in

the booth across from Bo.

"The regulars. Harvey Moore from Thrall. Zach Gibbons."

"Tom's daddy?"

"Not much of a one," Bo answered. He didn't care for Zach Gibbons. He spent Tom's paycheck from working at the Sinclair Station on too many beers.

"Harvey comes over from Thrall?"

"Every night. Thinks if he's over here, no one over there will know he's a drunk."

James made a note to have a watch put once again on Highway 27 for drunk drivers. "You didn't see or hear anything out of the ordinary."

"Nope."

"So you didn't slip out between customers and knock off Ernie Masterson 'cuz he was slappin' Pearl around?"

Bo kept his gaze steady on the table. "Nope."

"Didn't take out the man who was responsible for Maeve O'Day's death?"

"Nope."

"Didn't leave your bandanna in the home of the murdered man's wife?" James W. took pleasure in the fact that Bo's gaze hardened at that one. "Guess Pearl had more than one reason to not want Ernie around, huh?"

Bo took a measured breath. "Pearl's a good person, James W." He looked straight at the sheriff. "And you know it."

"That I do." James W. leaned forward. "Even nice people can be pushed into doin' somethin' bad if they think the situation warrants."

Bo studied the sheriff's face. He saw in it confirmation that James W. knew the story behind Bo's murder conviction. Killing the man who had raped his sister had been justified violence in Bo's eyes.

"I'm not your culprit, James W.," he said flatly. "Neither is Pearl."

James W. pulled a notepad out of his pocket. "That remains to be seen," he said matter-of-factly. "Let's go over this again."

Chapter Twenty-Five
Hush, Little Mamma

"It's turnin' into a long day," Elsbeth said. She smoothed the wine-colored sweater over her matching polyester pants and smothered a yawn.

"It's only noon." Pastor Matt Hayden looked out the hospital room's single window. "I'm tired enough for it to be midnight."

Miss Olivia's room in the Wilks Medical Clinic was small, allowing only for a chair on one side of the bed. Elsbeth sat in the chair while Pastor Hayden leaned against the window jamb. A monitor hung on the wall behind the bed, and Matt watched as the heartbeat, now steady but very weak, pulsed in green across the bottom of the screen. The blood-pressure lines in red suggested that Miss Olivia was nearing stroke proportions.

The only reason Miss Olivia wasn't in a hospital in Austin right now was that the roads were still covered with ice.

"Elsbeth?" Miss Olivia whispered.

"Miss Olivia." Elsbeth sat forward in her chair and touched

the old woman's fingers. Intravenous tubes protruded gruesomely from the hand's top.

"Pain," Miss Olivia said hoarsely and put her fist over heart.

"Now?" Matt became instantly alarmed.

"Last night." Miss Olivia closed her eyes. "You came."

"I'll always come, Miss Olivia. Me and James W. Do you want me to get him?"

Miss Olivia shook her head. "You were lookin' for Ernie," she said. "Last night. Did you find him?"

Elsbeth's eyes rounded in horror, but the look was quickly controlled. Matt almost missed it.

"Don't you worry about that, now Miss Olivia. You just take it easy so you can get stronger, you hear?"

"Ernie's a bad one," Miss Olivia said. She opened her eyes and looked at Elsbeth. "Never wanted to say it out loud before. Those questions you asked?"

"Forget about that, Miss Olivia," Elsbeth pleaded. "It's not important now." Matt could hear the urgency in her voice to change the subject. "Jimmy Jr. said he might get here a day early. Just to see you."

Miss Olivia seemed to settle down. A small smile hinted at her old, wrinkled mouth. "He's a good boy."

"He's gonna be governor," Elsbeth said with confidence.

"We'll make sure of that," Miss Olivia agreed. She closed her eyes, and this time Elsbeth looked relieved to see that the frail old woman relaxed enough to fall asleep.

"What was that all about?" Matt asked.

Elsbeth kept her gaze on her mother-in-law. "James W. said

not to tell Miss Olivia about Ernie until she's stronger." She pursed her lips then, and Matt knew she would answer no more questions. He studied the back of Elsbeth's head. For the first time since he'd met her, Elsbeth was silent.

"I think I'll head on back to the parsonage for some lunch," he said. "Chances are she won't wake up again for a while."

"You do that, Pastor," Elsbeth said, flashing him a smile. "Sure do appreciate your time. You don't have to come back."

Chapter Twenty-Six
Zach Gibbons

"Heard you questioned my boy this mornin'." Zach Gibbons, a scarecrow of a man, sat down in the chair across from the sheriff.

James W. was working at the Fire and Ice House's corner table by the wood stove. Richard Dube, having been relieved of phone duty at the office, sat beside the sheriff, drinking a hot chocolate. The lunch crowd was starting to arrive, and the scent of spicy, warm food filled the restaurant. The sheriff had given thought to moving his investigation to the police station after the power had come back on mid-morning, but the promise of Dorothy Jo Devereaux's shrimp and grits had chased away the idea until after lunch.

"Is my boy in some kind of trouble?" Zach persisted.

James W. looked at the sorry excuse for a man that sat across from him. Zach Gibbons' eyes were red from his drunk the night before. His face was unshaven and dirty. Richard Dube had actually slid his chair back to avoid the stench emanating from the man. Zach's plaid shirt was buttoned all the way to the collar in an attempt to look formal for his summons to the sheriff's presence.

"Only needed information from the boy," James W. reassured. "Same as I need information from you."

"What kind of information?" Zach snarled.

Like father, like son, James W. thought. Neither one of them liked the law or answering questions.

"What time did you get to the Fire and Ice House last night?"

Zach scratched his beard. "Same as always. Right after supper, I guess."

"Six or seven?" James W. prompted.

"Yeah. Somethin' like that."

James W. sighed. Specifics would not be easy to obtain from a man who spent most of his days in a drunken haze.

"Mind if I join you, Sheriff?"

James W. looked up to see Pastor Matt Hayden standing over the table. The look in the pastor's eye told the sheriff that the preacher had something on his mind.

James W. pulled out the last chair at the table. "Have yourself a seat, Reverend," he said. "This here's Zach Gibbons."

"Zach Gibbons?" Matt sat down. "Tom's dad? That's a fine young boy you've got there, Mr. Gibbons."

James W. shot a look at the preacher for telling the fib, but Matt just smiled and shrugged. The sheriff resumed his interrogation. "So you got here at your usual time and left when?"

"Closin'," Zach answered.

"Where'd you sit?"

"At the bar," Zach said. "Like to watch the TV."

"Who was workin' last night?"

"Bo." At least these short answers would make it easy for Richard to keep up with his notes, James thought. "What about Angie?"

"She went upstairs early."

"How early?" James W. pressed.

"Hell, I don't know." Zach frowned his annoyance. "Had to get ready for a date, I guess."

"What do you mean?"

"She came back downstairs a little while later. Right before the power went out."

James W. kept his gaze steady. "Angie left the bar last night?"

"Ain't no law against it," Zach replied with a sneer.

James W. felt Zach's contempt grow with each word the man said.

"The place wasn't busy," Zach continued. "Only me and Harvey. Fire kept us warm." He nodded toward the wood burning stove nearby. "Beer kept flowin'. Switched to bottles when the power went out. Bo chunked a coupla six packs in the ice."

"When did Angie come back?" James W. asked.

"A while later." Zach licked his lips. "Musta had a good time. Got herself a nice coat."

James W. noted that Matt had gone pale. Why? He'd have

to ask the preacher about that later. He turned his attention back to Zach. "Angie went out last night? Durin' the storm?"

"That's what I said. Ain't you got ears?"

"What about Bo? Did he leave at anytime last night?"

Zach considered. "Spent a lot of time in the kitchen," he said finally. "Had to wait for beers." He smiled, revealing two decayed front teeth. "Almost served myself once or twice."

James W. was quite certain the man had done exactly that.

"Bo could've left out the backdoor," Matt suggested.

Zach shook his head. "Naw. He was talkin' to a woman in the kitchen."

"A woman?" Richard Dube's head came up.

"Yeah. She was cryin'."

"I didn't know Bo had a girlfriend," James W. said.

Zach looked at the sheriff and laughed. "There's lots you don't know, Sheriff."

"Like what, Gibbons?"

"Like how Ernie got kicked out of this bar on Tuesday night." He looked meaningfully at Matt. "And why."

"Bo kicked Ernie out of the Fire and Ice House on Tuesday night?"

"Nope. Angie did. Said if she ever saw Ernie in her place again, she'd kill 'im." Gibbons grinned. "That's what this is about, ain't it Sheriff? Somebody killed ol' Ernie's sorry ass, and you think Bo did it." He leaned back in his chair, his eyes glowing with certain knowledge. "Well, you're after the wrong person, Sheriff Novak. Everybody knows Angie thought Ernie killed her ma. Threatened him with a knife in front of all of us.

She left here last night with a fire lit under her. So you go talk to the pretty redhead, Sheriff." His expression turned grim. "And you leave me and my son alone. Ya hear?"

***

"Simply because someone's got a temper doesn't mean they're a murderer, James W." Matt said, his voice low as the tables around them began to crowd. Richard Dube had gone to the bar to get another hot chocolate.

"She had motive. She had opportunity." James W. shook his head. "There's a black bandanna in my evidence room with grease on it that wouldn't wash out."

Matt felt a sickening feeling grow in his gut as he realized James W. was seriously considering Angie as a murder suspect. "It looked like you had somethin' to say when you came in," James W. said.

Matt looked puzzled for a moment, then he remembered. According to Miss Olivia, Elsbeth had been looking for Ernie last night. Before the murder.

Somehow bringing that up right now didn't seem like a good idea, Matt realized. James W. was on a scent. It was a wrong scent, but nonetheless, the sheriff didn't look in a listening mood about questioning a member of his own family about the murder.

"Your mamma woke up," Matt said instead. "I thought you'd want to know."

James W.'s expression immediately changed. "Miss Olivia?" James. W. looked hopeful. "Did she say anything?"

"She knew who Elsbeth and I were. Was happy that Jimmy Jr. is coming. All things considered, she looked pretty good."

James W. smiled. "I do appreciate your takin' care of things with my family while I carry on this investigation, Preacher. I'll never forget it."

"I'm glad to be of help," Matt said, then looked up as Angie approached the table. Her expression was grim.

"I think we'd better talk upstairs at your place," James W. said, rising from the table. "Thanks again, Preacher. I won't be needin' any more of your help just now."

Chapter Twenty-Seven
Too Hot to Swallow

Dismissed by a Novak for the second time that day, Matt watched as the threesome, Angie, James W. and Richard Dube, disappeared out the door that led to the back stairs.

Frustrated, Matt headed for the front door.

"You stayin' for lunch, Preacher?" Dorothy Jo Devereaux called out from behind the bar. "I made shrimp and grits today. Got some cornbread, too."

Matt considered. Waiting for him at home was a peanut butter sandwich. If he felt like splurging, he might even get up the energy to add some grape jelly. He took a deep whiff of the heavily scented air. God had not created him a fool. "Sounds too good to pass up, Dorothy Jo."

"I'll dish you up a bowl," she said, then looked at him. "Bo's in the kitchen eatin' lunch."

Matt met her gaze. "The sheriff had some questions for him earlier."

"Yep." Her smile was bitter. "I'll bet they'll try and hang this murder on him."

"James W. seems a fair man," Matt said.

She sniffed. "He's as fair as a Wilks gets, I suppose. Bo needs to watch out, though. I don't trust none of them."

"You worried about Bo?" Matt asked. When Dorothy Jo didn't answer, he nodded toward the kitchen. "How about I have that bowl of shrimp and grits in the back? I hate to see a man eat alone."

Though Matt didn't know her well, he would've sworn the wrinkled old woman looked relieved. He followed her into the kitchen, surprised at how familiar the setting felt. It had only been a week since he'd first stepped foot in the Fire and Ice House.

He sure hadn't been interested in starting a conversation with Bo on that day.

Matt waited while Dorothy Jo dished him up a bowl of the steaming white grits, set some shrimp on top and finished it off with a ladle of red sauce. She set his plate down across from Bo's, then turned to grab a half dozen corn bread muffins from the warmer and put them in a basket. "That'll do you boys for a while. I gotta go slice lemons." She left out through the swinging doors to the bar.

"Afternoon, Bo," Matt said as he sat down across from the bartender.

"Preacher." Today Bo's bandanna was blue.

"Guess this business with Ernie has a lot of people nervous," Matt said by way of opening.

"I'm not nervous." Bo's reply was flat.

"I was speaking of Dorothy Jo."

At that, Bo's mouth hinted at a smile. "She's a worrywart."

"Especially about you."

Bo spooned up another bite of grits. "Feelin's mutual."

"You, Dorothy Jo and Angie have created quite a little family here for yourselves." Matt shoveled in his first mouthful of the thick porridge.

His eyes rounded at the level of spice, and he swallowed quickly. Which was a mistake, he acknowledged immediately. He choked as the cayenne pepper ignited his throat on the way down.

Amused, Bo got to his feet and pulled a gallon of milk from the fridge. He handed it and a glass to the Preacher. "It's that red eye gravy that gives it the kick."

Matt downed half the gallon.

"Maeve was part of this family, too." Bo returned to his seat across from Matt.

"Do you believe Ernie killed her?"

Bo broke off a slab of bread and buttered it thickly before answering. "No."

"Why?"

Bo considered. "Ernie knew a lot of secrets. But he was a coward." He bit into the bread and chewed thoughtfully. "It takes guts to kill somebody. Even an old lady with Alzheimer's."

"Somebody's got to have a reason for doing something like that. Not just guts," Matt observed.

Bo shot a glance at the preacher before swallowing. "I figure that whoever drove Maeve out to that deer lease cared about the secrets Maeve had."

"Do you have any ideas who did kill Ernie?"

"Ernie knew a lot of things about a lot of people. He used that information to get stuff he wanted. Maybe he asked the wrong person for the wrong thing this time."

"Like what?"

"It's no fun doin' time for murder." Bo looked as though he were working the question through for the first time. "Maybe Ernie knew who drove Maeve O'Day out to the deer lease."

Matt considered the suggestion. The Sinclair Station *was* situated such that Ernie could see just about everything that happened in town. Matt scooped up another spoonful of grits, then eyed it with suspicion.

Bo smirked. "You didn't even bite into the shrimp yet. If the sauce doesn't get you, that breading will."

It was a challenge and Matt knew it. This time he was prepared for the kick that came with the bite and had a glass of milk ready. "How could Ernie know that?"

"He works in the center of town. Maybe he saw Maeve goin' into someone's house. Maybe he saw Shadow in the back of somebody's car." Bo shrugged. "All I know is that Ernie was a low-down piece of crap who'd blackmail anyone about anything."

"You didn't care much for Ernie." Proud he'd managed to swallow without choking, Matt reached for the cornbread.

"Couldn't stand him," Bo said casually. "He hassled Angie. He was a lousy husband."

"You know about him hitting Pearl, then."

"And his drinkin'. And his womanizin'. Pearl deserves better than him."

"You like Pearl."

"Mrs. Masterson is a lady." Bo's voice lowered appreciably and Matt knew he was treading on thin ice.

"I understand she didn't stay at her house last night," he pressed.

"Really." Bo rose abruptly from the table and took his dishes to the sink.

"Zach Gibbons said he heard a woman crying in the Ice House's kitchen last night."

Bo's back straightened. "You suggestin' somethin', Preacher?"

Matt looked at Bo's proximity to the knife rack and wondered exactly what means the ex-con had used to commit murder. "Nope. Not suggesting a thing."

"Good." Bo rinsed his dish in the sink and went out to tend the bar.

Chapter Twenty-Eight
Go to Jail

Friday morning brought a warm breeze to Wilks. Pastor Matt Hayden, fresh from a morning shower after a good night's sleep, marveled at the spring-like conditions as he walked from parsonage to church. Halfway down the path between the two buildings, he removed his windbreaker and slung it over his shoulders.

He'd finished Thursday on a happier note than he'd started it. He liked attending choir practice, though he didn't figure his voice added much to the men's section. Still, he enjoyed the people who laughed as much as they sang. He especially liked the desserts they ate when practice was finished.

Of course, talk last night had mostly been about Ernie Masterson. He couldn't help but notice that not one person had expressed any sorrow over Ernie's death. Horror, yes. Surprise, definitely. Regret, no.

Coming up with the sermon for Ernie's funeral would be an interesting task. Matt had spent most of Thursday afternoon with Pearl, helping her with arrangements. The funeral was to be the next day, Saturday. Matt was grateful this weekend would be Layman's Sunday. He didn't have to prepare sermons for two days in a row.

He hopped up the front steps of the church, two at a time, invigorated by the sixty-degree temperature. He whistled as he opened the front door, already unlocked because the church secretary began her duties promptly at eight every morning. The hour was now closer to nine.

"Good morning, Mrs. Fullenweider," he called out as he entered the dark lobby. He allowed his gaze to trail up to the steeple high above him, and wondered at the cost of installing windows to brighten the dreary interior.

"Good morning, Pastor Hayden," she said as he entered her outer office. Matt imagined Ann Fullenweider had been something of a catch in her younger days. Her hairstyle might have come straight from the fifties and her make-up was a little overdone, but her clothes were professional, and she had a style that reminded him of Jackie O. "You have a visitor," she said, her well-penciled eyebrows raised in interest.

"A visitor?" Matt echoed.

"I let her in your office. I hope you don't mind. She was so distraught—"

"Pearl Masterson?" Matt walked quickly toward his office and pushed open the door.

It wasn't Pearl who greeted him, however. Dorothy Jo Devereaux jumped to her feet as he entered. "Pastor Hayden."

"Dorothy Jo," he said in surprise.

"Pastor, you've got to do somethin'." Dorothy Jo wore a dress that looked like it hadn't been worn in years. She'd even pulled her long gray hair back and attempted to pile it on her head.

This was an official visit, Matt realized.

"What's wrong?" he asked.

"Sheriff Novak came last night. At ten o'clock."

"To your place?"

"No, no." She waved impatiently. "To the Fire and Ice House."

"What did he do?"

"That's what you've got to fix," Dorothy Jo said. She sat down hard in the chair. "I was afraid this was goin' to happen."

"He arrested Bo." Matt said, understanding dawning.

"No," Dorothy Jo sobbed. "Angie. He took Angie away and put her in jail for the murder of Ernie Masterson."

***

"Look, Preacher, this is police business. Everything checks out." James W. sat in the leather chair behind his large pine desk and glanced out the window of his second-story office. The Wilks County municipal building housed the sheriff's offices, the fire and utility agencies and the two-room basement jail. "I had to bring her in last night. I had reason to believe that she would attempt to flee the area."

Matt Hayden sat in the straight-back chair across from the sheriff's desk. "James W., I can't believe that Angie O'Day is responsible for Ernie Masterson's death."

"I got the coroner's report right here, Pastor. Maybe it started out more as an accident. The blow to Ernie's head wasn't that severe, but apparently, he did lose his balance and hit his head good against the bumper. Turning the ignition in that van, though, well, that makes it murder."

Matt shook his head. "Did the coroner have an estimate on the time of death?"

"He put it between nine and eleven p.m. I can make it closer than that. Ernie sold his last gallon of gas at ten-oh-five p.m.— to Ann Fullenweider, your secretary, I might add. Pearl found him at ten-thirty." James W. folded his hands over his stomach. "Angie O'Day left the Fire and Ice House before ten o'clock. She's got no alibi."

But she did, Matt thought frantically, and he was it. Why hadn't Angie told the sheriff that she had come to the parsonage?

"May I see her?" Matt asked.

James W. let out a frustrated sigh. "Why do you insist on getting involved in this? People don't want their minister goin' to a bar for lunch. They don't cotton to preachers hangin' around with the likes of those that hang around bars. Hell, I'm a fair man, and I'm beginning to wonder if you've got a thing for that girl."

"Jesus broke bread with the people who were considered unworthy," Matt reminded him.

James W. blinked. "You're tryin' to evangelize her?"

Knowing it would get him into Angie's cell, Matt lied. "Yes."

Chuckling, the sheriff rose from his chair. "I'll let you in, then," he said. "Watch I don't have to charge Angie with another murder besides Ernie's."

***

"What are you doing here?" Angie O'Day sat across from Matt in the small conference room. Her face was redder than her hair and her hands were fisted on the table. Matt couldn't tell if she was angry, embarrassed, or both.

"I came to talk some sense into you," Matt said. He knew darn well *he* was angry.

"Sense?" She glanced nervously at the window in the room's door. "Sense?" she repeated, lowering her voice. "You of all people have no right to talk to me about sense. Do you know what your congregation would say if they knew you were in here right now?"

He couldn't sit. He was too angry to sit. He pushed away from the table and paced. "Angie, you were with me when Ernie Masterson was murdered. Why haven't you told that to the sheriff?"

Angie shook her head. "And you were goin' to talk to me about sense."

"I'm going to talk to you about truth. As in telling it. If you don't, I will."

"No, you won't," she said sharply. "I was there for spiritual advice. You can't betray that confidence."

"Spiritual advice, my foot," Matt snapped. "You came over to find out why I thought your mother was murdered."

"I didn't stay there the whole time that Ernie might have been killed. Even if I did tell James W. I was at your place, I still would have had time to go over to the Sinclair Station and bop Ernie over the head."

"Angie—"

"No, listen! Why risk your reputation when it wouldn't do any good, anyway?"

Matt finally sat in the chair across from her. "It's not something I'm ashamed of."

"You should be. A single man havin' drinks with a suspected whore is bad enough. When that single man's a preacher—hell, Preacher, this town will crucify you."

"Angie, that's not the issue here."

"Yes, it is." She banged her fist on the table, then immediately shoved it into her lap. "Do you think I killed Ernie Masterson?"

"I know you didn't," Matt said with conviction.

"Then you have to have faith that the truth will come out." Angie lowered her voice and calmed her breathing. "The truth will come out," she repeated. "Somebody did kill Ernie. When I find out who it was, I'll probably shake their hand. But I didn't do it, and I know I'll be found innocent."

Matt stared at her. His faith was in God, but she was putting her faith in people. Somehow her faith seemed as naive to him as he was sure his faith seemed to her.

That was something to consider.

"I come from a cop family, remember?" he said.

She nodded.

"I know how these things go. Once they've got one suspect, they stop looking for others. They spend all their time and effort trying to convict the bird they have in hand."

"Then I guess you'll have to do the lookin', Preacher. For now, anyway. I'm not goin' to give that church a reason for ditchin' the first good pastor they've ever had."

Matt swallowed hard at the compliment. "You're giving me too much responsibility," he said. "You need to put the facts before James W."

"Yeah, I'm givin' you plenty of responsibility. If you don't think the sheriff'll look for the truth, you find it and give it to him."

Matt felt like swearing for the first time in months, but he fought off the urge. "Don't do this to me, Angie."

She sat back in her chair. "I'm the one in jail, remember? What am I doin' to you?"

"You're . . . different." He swallowed hard. "You're not one of my parishioners."

"What does that have to do with this?"

"I don't want to be responsible for you. Not like that."

"What do you want, then?"

Matt stood abruptly. "This is ridiculous."

"No." Angie's voice was quiet, but firm. "Face it, Preacher. You feel different about me than you do anybody else. That's how I feel about you. It's there between us. A match that's waitin' to be lit."

"Damn you." He went to the door but didn't knock to be let out.

Angie's mouth twitched. "Would that be to hell, Preacher? Is that where you want me to go?"

"No." He didn't turn from the door.

"Is that why you came in here today and told me to throw your career out the window to save my skin?"

"No."

"Then what do you want?"

He shrugged. It was useless fighting any longer. He knew the truth as well as she did. He turned. "You."

Her smile wasn't victorious, nor coy. It was shy, like a flower whose bloom first touches sun. The vulnerability in her soft eyes ripped through him.

"I don't trust people very much," she whispered. "But I trust you. Get me out, Matt. Please."

He wanted to touch her, to hold her, to take the fear out of her gaze and kiss away her sadness. He knew she wanted the same. He could feel it in her breathing as it quickened when he stepped nearer.

She drew back, however, darting a quick glance at the door's window. "They're comin'," she said under her breath.

He held his hand out to her, and she took it. It was a simple touch, yet the sensation of her skin against his sent a rush of warmth up his arm. He'd never figured a woman as strong as Angie would have such a delicate hand.

The door behind Matt opened, and Richard Dube stuck his head in the small conference room. "Time's up."

"Thanks for the visit, Preacher," she said, squaring her shoulders. "Don't come around again. I won't see you."

Matt gave her hand a squeeze before walking away. When he turned to her from the doorway, his gaze was dark. "You won't have a choice."

Chapter Twenty-Nine
Pastor Osterburg

Matt Hayden got behind the wheel of his aging Ford Tempo and turned the ignition. He felt like he'd been sucker-punched. He stared at the county municipal building blindly, seeing neither the tan brick of its exterior nor the United States and Texas flags that blew evenly from their poles.

Nor did he see James W. staring down at him from the sheriff's second-story window.

Finally, Matt put the car into reverse and edged out of the parking lot. By rote he drove past the square and across the bridge to Grace's paved lot. He parked in front of the church but didn't get out.

The responsibility he felt on his shoulders was huge. He had neither the energy nor the inclination to go into his office and start on a sermon eulogizing Ernie Masterson. The business of the last week had gotten out of hand. Way out of hand. He had to put an end to it. Maeve's disappearance, her mortal wound, her funeral, Ernie's murder, Miss Olivia's heart attack, and now Angie's arrest.

Two months ago he hadn't even known these people. Now it seemed as though their justice rested on his shoulders.

Funny, he thought. He'd become a pastor to escape the need for justice in the case of his father's death. Angie had been halfway right about that on Wednesday night. Becoming a pastor might have been a bit of a cop-out for him. He'd seen it as a solution. Loving God released Matt from anger, giving him a purpose that still served mankind.

But now, loving God would put him in a position to look for justice all over again. Only this time he would do so not to manifest hate, but to show love.

He leaned his head against the steering wheel. So many questions. About himself. About the facts. Where could he start to prove Angie's innocence?

"You look at the gray," Miss Olivia had said. "Then the black and white becomes obvious."

Matt put the car into reverse. At least he knew where to begin fulfilling his responsibilities. Plenty of questions needed answering. Issues needed clarification. He'd start with the questions of three days ago and work his way forward.

He put the car in drive, listened to it grumble at the order and prayed it would get him to and from Houston in one piece.

***

Matt had the good sense to call ahead to Pastor Fred Osterburg. His old professor not only gave him an appointment, but directions through the tree-lined streets of the University of St. Thomas area.

Matt parked his car and listened to it cough as he turned off the engine. He might make it back to Wilks, and he might not. He slammed the door shut, studied the red brick building before him and jogged up its cement steps.

Pastor Osterburg was waiting at the top of the stairs. Matt smiled at the slightly built man with the Lincoln-trimmed beard and hearty laugh.

"Matt Hayden." Pastor Osterburg's bass voice resonated. "This is a pleasure."

"The pleasure is mine." Matt smiled and shook the pastor's extended hand. "Thank you for making time in your schedule to see me."

"It's a beautiful Friday for a walk, don't you think?" Pastor Osterburg said, surveying the blue, cloudless sky. "Let me show you St. Thomas."

Matt cheerfully walked along as the spry, older man led him around the campus. Though seventy years of age, Fred Osterburg was ageless. His hair was still mostly black, his steps easy. Their walk encompassed half a mile at least of park-lined sidewalks and landscaped walkways. Outside the walls of the campus, the busy traffic of metropolitan Houston zoomed by.

"You didn't come here to talk about the university," Pastor Osterburg said as they finished their circle of the quad. "You came here to ask me some questions. How are things in Wilks?"

Matt cleared his throat. "Fine, Pastor."

The old man threw his head back and laughed. "Wilks is a little town with big issues," he said knowingly. "Things are seldom *fine*. And you can call me Fred. I'm not your professor any longer."

***

Fred Osterburg's office was on the third floor of Hovey Hall, overlooking the quad. A small, functional room, it held an oak desk and two chairs and a couple of bookshelves on either side of the lone window, none of which matched. Apparently, the University of St. Thomas spent little effort in furnishing the offices of their visiting professors, Matt thought.

"Maeve O'Day," Pastor Osterburg said, shaking his head. "Strong-willed woman. Hate to hear that's how she died."

"It was gruesome," Matt agreed.

"She had a child, a daughter, I think." Fred leaned back in his wood chair.

"Angie. Angel O'Day."

"That's right." Fred's chair came down with a thud. "Maeve opened the Fire and Ice House when she was expecting her baby." The old pastor grinned. "It being directly across the river from the church sure lit a fire under a few members."

"Not you, though," Matt could plainly see.

Fred shrugged. "Maeve O'Day's place fed more hungry folk than Grace ever did."

"Not all of the members of Grace look at it that way."

"No." Fred's expression sobered. "Some of them are downright unpleasant. That little girl, one time she came to Sunday School." He shook his head. "I didn't hear about it until afterward. I taught the adult class, you see. I went over there to apologize." He puffed out his cheeks and Matt knew the incident still bothered him. "Maeve O'Day met me at the door with a butcher knife. Can't say as I blamed her."

Matt suppressed a smile. Fred Osterburg confirmed all the stories he'd heard about Maeve O'Day.

"I understand you went to all of the city council meetings when you were at Wilks."

"Involvement in that community is important," Fred said with a nod. "Are you thinking of doing the same?"

"Perhaps," Matt allowed. "But I was wondering if you were at the meeting where they opened the bids for the old firehouse. When Maeve O'Day bought the place."

Again, Fred's smile flashed. "Most of the people in that room were related to the Wilks in one way or another. Or employed by them. There was quite a furor." He chuckled.

"Yet, Maeve O'Day managed to get a liquor license out of that same city council."

Pastor Osterburg frowned. "I guess she did." He thought hard, then looked up somewhat surprised. "It passed without a vote against it that I can remember."

"Doesn't that strike you as odd?" Matt asked.

"Guess so." Fred scratched at his beard. "There was so much going on at the time. Our people had been taken hostage in Iran. TV thought it would be over so soon they made the mistake of having a nightly special about it and numbering the days. Around two hundred, there wasn't much more to say. Then we found out about Roth. Cash disappeared. I guess having a bar across the river didn't faze me."

"The community must have been stunned."

Fred's expression grew grim. "One of the worst times in my pastoral career. Tragic."

"Miss Olivia took it pretty hard, I understand."

"Now there's a strong woman." Fred punched the air with his forefinger. "The Marines called me with the news about Roth. Asked me to go with their representative over to the mansion to tell the family."

The older man shook his head. "I remember that petite little woman opening the door. She was dressed all in black. All I could think of was that we were about to make her life a thousand times worse."

Matt nodded. Even now, Fred Osterburg looked older at the telling of the story.

"She took the news of Roth's death with such dignity. Her back straight as a rod. She kept a control of her emotions that I didn't know a person could keep. She was silent for an entire five minutes after we told her. I watched the time tick by on the mantel clock." Fred shook his head. "When she finally spoke, her voice was so quiet we could hardly hear her. She asked me if we had told Pearl yet, and I said no, and she said I should bring Pearl to the mansion after I gave her the news." Fred sighed deeply. "I thought that was pretty decent of Miss Olivia. In her opinion, Roth had married beneath his station. That had been quite a bone of contention between Miss Olivia and Cash, I can tell you."

"So you left Miss Olivia's to tell Pearl about Roth's death."

"Yes. I ran by the Sinclair Station to let Ernie know Miss Olivia wanted him to come over, then I went to tell Pearl."

Matt frowned. "Miss Olivia asked you to get Ernie Masterson?"

Fred nodded. "To go find Cash, I presume. Those two were thicker than mud." He wiped a speck of dust off his desk. "Ernie finally found Cash in Houston. Told Cash to come home."

"Cash was quite a personality, I understand."

"Got into more mischief than Miss Olivia deserved," Fred said. "He was a popular man in Texas with the legislators. I guess he had like three days of meetings with all of 'em at the time of the Houston debate. Made you wonder what he did to make them so friendly."

"How long did they search for Cash before they figured he was dead?"

"Two weeks hard out. Then a few more weeks, with the Texas Rangers coming in and all. A long time went by before Miss Olivia agreed with James W. that they should have some sort of memorial for him."

"How did Miss Olivia handle everything?"

"Odd, that. She seemed more . . . resolved . . . than mournful. I tried to counsel her about Cash's disappearance, but she'd hold up her hand and tell me that Pearl needed my care more than she did. After a bit, I stopped bringing it up."

Matt stood. "I thank you for your time, Fred."

The professor studied him carefully. "I've answered a question for you, but I'm not sure what you asked."

Matt smiled. "I'll be coming to Houston again soon. We'll talk."

Chapter Thirty
Elsbeth Novak

Matt returned to Wilks late that afternoon. His Tempo had overheated twice on the trip back from Houston, confirming his fears that he'd have to find a different vehicle before the hot Texas summer arrived.

He drove past Ernie's Sinclair Station, checked his watch, then steered directly for Sheriff Novak's ranch home on the north side of town.

The drive took a little under seven minutes.

He parked under the redbud tree in the front drive and walked up the flagstone path to the front porch. James W. must not do so bad for himself, Matt thought, taking in the sprawling house that overlooked the Colorado River. When he rang the doorbell, he was greeted by a melody of chimes that he was sure was intended to impress visitors to the Novak ranch.

"Reverend Hayden," Elsbeth said in surprise as she pulled open the heavy front door. "Come in."

Matt stepped into the marble-tiled entranceway. Elsbeth led the way into the elegant, wide front room.

Ladies' clothes were strewn over every chair and divan.

"Pardon the mess," Elsbeth said, pushing a navy blue dress to the side and gesturing the pastor toward an overstuffed chair. "Jimmy Jr. is coming to town for Ernie's funeral, and I want to be ready."

Ready for the media that followed the gubernatorial candidate, Matt thought, but kept his musing to himself.

"What brings you out here?" she asked, busily stacking shoeboxes against the stone fireplace.

"I had a few questions I'd like to ask you in private."

"Oh?" She ran a hand through her wavy brown hair. Matt noted she must have spent the morning at the beauty shop. Her hair was browner and wavier than the last time he'd seen it.

"I was surprised to see you at Maeve O'Day's funeral the other day."

"I might say the same for you." Elsbeth turned the conversation quickly. Her eyes sharpened, and her speech pitched higher. "I should think that a pastor would stay away from associating with the friends of that kind of person."

Matt wouldn't be put off the scent. "All the more reason you can imagine my surprise at seeing you sitting in the back row of the church."

Elsbeth settled herself on the couch across from Matt. He wondered if her strategic placement wasn't intentional. With the sun streaming through the window behind her, he could not discern Elsbeth's reaction to his query.

After a moment's pause, Elsbeth let out a humorless chuckle. "I guess we both felt sorry for the poor old woman."

Matt pressed his lips together. He'd figured this would be a difficult interrogation. He'd been right.

"Did you learn what you came to find out?" he asked.

"What could I possibly want to know about that woman?" Elsbeth shuddered. "Really, Reverend Hayden, you're makin' too much out of my bein' there."

"Perhaps," Matt allowed. "But if you didn't get your answer at Maeve's funeral, perhaps you thought Ernie might have been able to help you. Was that why you were looking for him Wednesday night?"

Elsbeth stood, turning her back full on Matt. He took that as a sign that he was getting close to the truth.

"I don't remember thinking about Ernie Wednesday night."

"You called Pearl, looking for Ernie. And Miss Olivia."

"Perhaps I did." When she turned, her face was lit in a bright smile. "Now I remember. My car wasn't working, and I wanted to tell Ernie he needed to come out Thursday morning and fix it."

"Your car was working. You were in your car when you used your cell," Matt reminded her. "Pearl said that it was breaking up pretty bad with the thunderstorm."

"Hmm." She mused quietly, then picked up a purple wool suit and held it up to the mirror. "Perhaps I was on my way to Miss Olivia's. That was the night of her heart attack, as you well know."

"I know you're not telling me everything." Matt stood. "If

you'd rather I take this up with James W.—"

"No!" Elsbeth dropped the suit unceremoniously on the chair. "There's no reason to bring James W. into this."

"Then perhaps you can clear up why you wanted to see Ernie Masterson so badly that evening, and why you were at Maeve O'Day's funeral that day." Matt sat back down.

"I had no love for Maeve O'Day," Elsbeth said. "I wanted to see who else would show at her funeral, that's all."

Matt studied her face. Somewhere along the line, Elsbeth was telling him the truth. Cryptically, but telling it nonetheless. "What was the reason you were looking for Ernie?"

Elsbeth closed her lips firmly.

"There's a woman in jail for a crime she did not commit," he said. "I think you're a material witness, if not more, Mrs. Novak. Either you answer my questions now, or we go down and discuss this with James W."

She studied her hands, the wall, the carpet. Anything but Matt's face.

"You're my pastor."

"Obviously."

"You can't reveal what we talk about. Ethically, I mean," she said nervously.

"Not unless you want me to." He nodded. "Or unless you've committed a crime."

Elsbeth turned toward the window, crossed her arms over her midsection, and watched the breeze blow through the redbud trees for a long moment. "All right," she said, "I'll tell you." She walked back to the couch. "But you do not have my permission to discuss this with anyone. Do you understand?"

Matt nodded. "As long as you haven't done anything wrong."

"I have a son runnin' for governor, and I don't even know all of the skeletons in my closet." She sat down. "I deserve the truth."

"The truth about what, Elsbeth?"

"Whether or not my husband is Angie O'Day's father."

Matt kept his gaze steady, though the feeling of shock he was experiencing was hard to keep off his face. "You think James W. fathered Angie?"

"Yes," she said, with a breath of relief. "I've wanted to say that for thirty-five years. Finally, it's out."

"Maybe you'd better tell me about it." Matt settled in his chair.

"I don't blame James W. With a father like Cash, bringing those prostitutes over to the mansion to conduct their business when Miss Olivia was gone..." Elsbeth shook her head.

"Cash brought Lida's girls to his house?"

"Saw it with my own eyes."

"How does any of that make James W. Angie's father?"

"When news got out that Maeve O'Day was pregnant—I mean, anyone who worked at Miss Lida's Rose Hotel risked a bun in the oven, right?" Elsbeth stood and paced toward the fireplace mantel. "But when that woman showed up to Cash's memorial service . . . ."

"What woman?"

"Maeve O'Day. Showing plenty, I can tell you. Back then,

well, women didn't go out when you showed that much."

"Maeve O'Day was pregnant and she went to your father-in-law's funeral?"

She nodded. "Miss Olivia didn't say a word. It was the first and only time I've ever seen Miss Olivia look scared."

"Of Maeve O'Day?"

"Yes. Only for a moment. Later when the cars were lining up for the procession to the cemetery, Maeve came out of the church. Miss Olivia and James W. were waiting for the limousine to swing around. Maeve and Miss Olivia just stared at each other. Then the limo came. When she got in that car, Miss Olivia looked like she'd seen a ghost."

"They had a burial? With no body?"

"It was a memorial service, really."

"How long after Cash disappeared?"

Elsbeth puzzled the question for a moment. "Five, maybe six months? I mean, Cash wasn't officially declared dead for years. But Miss Olivia wanted closure. She put an empty casket in the ground with some of Cash's things in it. Said she needed the ritual so that she could get on with her life. We had a luncheon at the house afterwards. Just like a real funeral."

"Did Maeve O'Day come over to the house after the service?"

Elsbeth shook her head. "No, but her message had been delivered just the same."

"Message?"

"Blackmail. I think Maeve O'Day wanted the Wilks' money to keep her mouth shut about James W. fatherin' her baby."

"Miss Olivia had her heart attack right after the memorial service," Matt said.

"She didn't have her heart attack that day," Elsbeth corrected him. "It was two days later. I'll never forget that, I can tell you."

"You were with her?" Matt prodded.

"James W. and I were starting to get serious about each other by then," Elsbeth said. "Miss Olivia had invited me over to a Bible Study so her friends could get to know me. Talk about walking a gauntlet! Anyway, the mail man came by, Miss Olivia answered the door, did a quick look through the mail, opened one letter, then boom! Fell right over in the hallway. Near to where she fell Wednesday night."

"Was there something in the mail that upset her?"

"Now, that was the silliest thing," Elsbeth replied. "One of the letters, the one in her hand when she fell, all it had in it was a coupon for toilet paper. And the return address said it was from Maeve O'Day."

"Toilet paper," Matt repeated.

"No note, no nothin'. Just the coupon."

"So as far as you know, Maeve O'Day never got any kind of money from Miss Olivia."

"She got her money, all right. From Cash."

Matt sat forward. "Cash?"

"Do you think it was a coincidence that Maeve O'Day had enough money to buy the firehouse?" Elsbeth huffed. "Besides, I saw Ernie doing Cash's business for him at Lida's Rose Hotel with my very own eyes."

"When?"

"Right before news came about Roth's being killed. Football season was long gone, and prom wasn't for another month," Elsbeth said. "Us girls were lookin' for somethin' to do."

"*You* went to Miss Lida's?"

"I was a senior in high school. It was a dare." Elsbeth shrugged. "We thought, us girls thought, that maybe some of the football players would go over to Miss Lida's. Girl stuff. In Texas, high school is all about football, and high school girls are all about football players. We were in the woods behind the parkin' lot."

"What did you see?"

"Ernie Masterson drove up in Cash's car. And guess who was in the back seat? Maeve O'Day. You know what that means." She shot Matt a superior look. "And after Ernie got Maeve into Miss Lida's, he went back to the car for a little suitcase, and he took that in, too. When he came out, he was empty-handed."

"I don't understand."

"Wilks is located smack between Austin and Houston. I think Cash threw a little party at the mansion for his legislative buddies when everyone was passing through on their way to the debate."

"Where was Miss Olivia?"

Elsbeth shot Matt a withering look. "Well, not there, obviously. Cash would've made sure she wasn't home."

"And you think that's the night when Maeve O'Day let Cash know that James W. had gotten her pregnant."

"It follows, doesn't it? They talked after the party. Then Ernie drove her home and paid her off with a suitcase full of money."

"And you still went ahead and married this man?"

Elsbeth bowed her head. "James W. was a kid. Every boy in town went over to Lida's at some time. It was almost a right of passage." She looked up sharply. "But all that was before he and I started seeing each other. There's no doubt in my mind he's been faithful to me ever since."

"That's a heckuva stretch to make between Ernie driving Cash's car, taking Maeve back to Lida's and James W. fathering a child." Matt shook his head. "I don't see it."

"Don't forget the suitcase full of money! Besides, James W.'s always championed her. He goes over to that Fire and Ice House 'most every day. He says he's checking for health violations, but that's what the county has a health inspector for, isn't it? He defended that little girl when Miss Olivia kicked her out of Sunday School." Elsbeth's tone turned bitter. "Oh, he cares about Angie O'Day. Make no mistake."

"He's arrested her for murder," Matt said.

"Didn't have much of a choice." Elsbeth turned her nose in the air. "Don't think he feels good about it, Pastor. How could he? If he'd been a good father, Angie wouldn't have turned out the way she did."

"So you figure Ernie was making a blackmail payment for Cash that night."

"Of course. Cash and Ernie were thick as thieves."

Matt shook his head to clear it. "Back to present day. Did

you talk to Ernie? Wednesday night?"

Elsbeth looked down at her hands, realizing that she'd been wringing them. She forced them open, spreading them over her knees. "Yes."

"Tell me about it."

"I walked in just before the cloudburst. Lord, I thought the wind was goin' to blow the door in."

"Ernie was in the office?"

"No. Back with the cars. The church van, actually."

"Go on."

"I asked him. Point-blank. Was James W. the father of Angie O'Day."

"What did Ernie say?"

"Nothing at first. He just laughed. Laughed so hard I wanted to hit him." Her eyes rounded with horror as she realized what she'd said. "But I didn't," she said quickly. "I asked him what was so funny." She bowed her head. "He didn't answer—not my question, anyway. He said he was going to make a killin' on this one. Those were his words exactly."

"Did he say anything else?"

"He told me he'd call me on Thursday if he remembered anything more."

Matt shook his head. "Buying time to blackmail someone, I'd wager."

"When I left that garage, Preacher, I swear he was alive. I couldn't have been there more than five minutes. Then when I was walkin' back in the house here, the phone was ringing. It was Pearl, saying she'd found Ernie in the garage. Dead."

Chapter Thirty-One
The Devil's in the Details

The sun was setting on a very long day when Matt walked into Grace Lutheran half an hour later. "Mrs. Fullenweider," Matt said in surprise.

She grinned. "Our Friday bulletin folding volunteers are not exactly available." She smoothed her too-black hair back with vibrant red-painted fingernails. "There's two services' worth of bulletins to fold. Somebody's got to do it."

"The funeral tomorrow and Sunday morning," Matt said as he realized. "We should have made some phone calls."

"It's no problem." Ann Fullenweider waved him off. "I've had some time to think things over," she said and let out a huff. "I've decided I need to get some things off my chest."

Matt turned from his office doorway. "To me?"

The secretary pushed back from the desk and faced him. "There's a lot of things that have happened in this town that people don't know the truth of. They think they do, but they don't." Mrs. Fullenweider furrowed her brow. "I've not said anything, 'cuz what I learn in this office is sacred, as far as I'm concerned."

Matt nodded. "And I've learned to appreciate that about you."

"I think if you knew . . . well, I don't think Angie O'Day killed Ernie Masterson," she rushed out, and dropped her gaze to the floor.

"I agree with you." He studied her bowed head. "What's on your mind?"

"I was at Ernie Masterson's Wednesday night buying gas. Right before the storm broke."

Matt nodded for her to continue.

"I saw Angie O'Day leave the Fire and Ice House. But she didn't go over to the gas station."

"You're right, Mrs. Fullenweider," Matt said, understanding dawning. "She came over to the parsonage."

The secretary's gaze was steady. "That's right, Reverend."

"She needed to talk about her mother," Matt said truthfully. "We talked for quite a while."

She studied him silently.

"I hope you can believe that," he continued. "But, either way, I know she didn't kill Ernie Masterson, and I've tried to convince her to tell the sheriff where she was. Angie won't listen to reason. She thinks it will ruin my reputation."

Slowly she nodded her head. "Angie's right." Then, deciding, she added, "I believe you, Reverend. And call me Ann, for Pete's sake."

Matt offered his hand. "Thanks, Ann."

"You're welcome." She shook his hand. "So let's get to work." Ann opened her purse and pulled out her keys.

"Do you have an idea who did kill Ernie?"

"I think this town has secrets that are generations old," she said slowly. "I know Pastor Osterburg kept files that documented more than baptisms and marriages. So have all the pastors since him." She crossed to the locked file cabinet and opened it. She sorted through the files, pulling out specific ones as she went. She turned toward the pastor and held them out for him to take. "If there's anything about the past that links up with this murder, my guess is you'll find the answer in these, Reverend Hayden."

***

By midnight, Matt had sorted through the files and made his chronological list of the events that had been confusing him.

Miss Olivia was right. If a person started out confused, asking questions and using logic brought out the black and white.

In this case, however, the black and white was painfully condemning.

He sat alone in his church office, a single lamp on the old scarred desk illuminating his work. He picked up the file on top of the stack and opened it.

"James Johann (Cash) Novak," it read. Matt chuckled humorlessly. Even the nickname had made it into the official church record. "Born November 11, 1921," the file went on. "Baptized December 6, 1921. Missing April 25, 1980.

Officially pronounced dead May 7, 1987. Death certificate signed by Danny Don Dube." The file held a black-and-white military photograph of a very young Cash Novak dressed in a Korean War uniform. Matt also found a copy of the marriage certificates to his first wife, Geneva Yeck, and another dated ten years later to Miss Olivia.

Matt put the file down and opened the next one. "Roth Johann Novak," it read. "Born September 19, 1944. Died April 24, 1980. Buried with honors, United States Army, Purple Heart." Again, the file contained a photograph of the soldier, this one in color. Roth Novak, freckled with buzzed red hair, smiled handsomely.

Pearl's first husband was significantly better looking than Ernie Masterson was, Matt thought. And cleaner.

He closed the folder and opened a third. "Olivia Johanna Wilks Novak," it read. He ran a finger down her biographical data. It listed the dates of her birth, her baptism, her confirmation and marriage. As with her house, the folder held no pictures.

It did contain, however, the agreement that had joined the assets of the Wilks and Novak families upon her marriage to Cash.

He closed the folder and bowed his head. How long would it be before he filled in the date of death in her folder? Feeling the weight of the world on his shoulders, he turned out the light and headed for home.

Chapter Thirty-Two
The Hospital Visit

Saturday morning was breezy and cool, but the sun shone and the birds sang in the live oaks that lined Mason Street.

Pastor Matt Hayden noticed neither as he walked the three blocks to the Wilks Medical Clinic. His steps were slow, his heart heavy. He'd found no respite in sleep the previous night. Prayer had been difficult, because he hadn't known what to pray for. Ignorance? Silence? Compassion? Courage?

In the end, he'd finally learned the true blessing in the wording of the Lord's Prayer. "Thy will be done," Matt had prayed over and over again. He didn't have a clue as to what he would will for himself, given the power.

Before he was ready to face what was to come, Matt forced himself up the cracked sidewalk of the Wilks Medical Clinic. The family of Miss Olivia was in the waiting room, dressed and ready for Ernie's funeral, but for the one task yet to perform. They had to tell their matriarch that Ernie Masterson was dead.

For once, James W. was not in uniform. He wore a black

suit and starched blue shirt. Elsbeth, in navy paisley, stood beside him. Jimmy Jr., impeccable in his white shirt, dark gray suit and tie, stood closest to Miss Olivia's hospital room door.

Pearl, dressed in black suit and gloves, was the lone person sitting in the room. Her eyes were red, her hands folded in her lap.

Matt let out a heavy sigh.

"Thank you for comin'." James W. walked forward and extended his hand.

Matt inclined his head, shook the burly sheriff's hand, then gestured toward Miss Olivia's room. "Has the doctor been in to see her this morning?"

Elsbeth, her gaze darting nervously toward the preacher and then back at the floor, nodded. "He said her vitals were steady enough to tell her about Ernie's passing." Elsbeth shook her head. "But the long run doesn't look good."

"We're not to go into much detail." Pearl's voice was almost a whisper. "She's to be upset as little as possible."

"Are you sure you want to be a part of this, Aunt Pearl?" Jimmy Jr. stepped forward.

"She'll want to see me at any rate," Pearl said, tearfully. "She's always been so good to me, and the doctor said she doesn't have long."

Matt swallowed hard but kept his silence. James W. went to the hospital room door, knocked softly, and peeked in. "You up to seein' visitors, Miss Olivia?"

The reply must have been in the positive, as James W. opened the door more widely and admitted the group into the cramped room.

James W. gestured to the only chair in the room for Pearl, and she more sank into it than sat on it. Elsbeth went to stand closest to Miss Olivia on her right, James W. on her left. Matt and Jimmy Jr. took the two corners at the foot of the bed.

Miss Olivia looked frail. Her skin was sunken, her breathing shallow. She'd had the nurse apply a touch of make-up at her cheeks and lips, but the color highlighted the paleness of her skin. She wore a lace-trimmed pink and blue bed jacket, which looked out of place with all of the wires that protruded from her chest and hands and nose.

"You all look like you're dressed for a funeral." Miss Olivia attempted a smile. "Hope it's not mine."

"Miss Olivia," Elsbeth started first, but James W. put out a hand.

"Mamma," he said softly, bending over the bed so his face was close to his mother's.

She looked at him. "You haven't called me Mamma for a long time," she said.

"I've got some bad news," James W. continued. "Mamma, Ernie's dead."

Matt trained his gaze on the monitor that blipped above Miss Olivia's head. The heart beat that pulsed weakly across the screen remained steady.

"Dead?" Miss Olivia echoed.

"He died Wednesday night, Miss Olivia," Elsbeth said gently. "The night you had your heart attack."

Miss Olivia looked from one face to another. "So you are dressed for a funeral."

"We wanted you to know," James W. said. "The doctor didn't give the okay until this morning."

Miss Olivia turned her head toward Pearl and reached for her hand. "My poor dear," she said quietly.

Pearl took the old woman's hand, and a tear slipped down her cheek. "Thank you, Miss Olivia," she whispered.

"You don't need to worry about a thing, Pearl. I'll take care of you," Miss Olivia said.

"You always have." Pearl lowered her head in a quiet sob.

"How did he die?" Miss Olivia asked.

"I think we've upset you enough without going into the details," Elsbeth said, casting a meaningful glance toward James W.

"I don't want details. Just how Ernie died," Miss Olivia insisted. She looked at her son, expecting an answer.

"He was killed, Mamma." James W. bowed his head. "Murdered."

This time the blip on the monitor above Miss Olivia's head did jump. "Who?"

Jimmy Jr. cleared his throat. "Angie O'Day's been arrested for the murder."

Matt watched the heart monitor blip wildly, and James W. shot an angry glare at his son.

"Angie?" Miss Olivia repeated.

"I had a question for you about that, Miss Olivia," Matt finally spoke.

Miss Olivia met his solid gaze, and for one unflinching moment, she held him stare for stare. "Yes?"

"I was wondering if you thought that was right?"

She stared at him, and in her face Matt witnessed the change. Lying before him was no longer the invalid Miss Olivia, but the force-to-be-reckoned-with Miss Olivia. Matt allowed himself a moment of admiration for her strength.

"How much do you know?" Miss Olivia whispered.

"Everything you did was logical," Matt said softly. "Once I looked at the gray, it was easier to see the black and white."

Miss Olivia nodded. She closed her eyes and took a deep breath, as if summoning all of her strength. When she opened them, she looked straight at James W. "You're wrong about arrestin' Angie O'Day," she said.

James W. shook his head. "Angie had motive. She thought Ernie killed her ma. She had opportunity. No one knows where she was at the time Ernie was killed. And Lord knows, she has the disposition."

"Disposition?" Miss Olivia repeated wearily. "Yes, I suppose I contributed to that." She glanced out the window. "The doctor says I'm likely not goin' to recover from this."

"You've proved them wrong before," Elsbeth said.

"Not this time." Miss Olivia shook her head. "Maybe that's as it should be." She looked at Matt. "What are you goin' to do?"

Matt sighed. "I'm not entirely sure . . ." He met her gaze straight on. "I do know that allowing an innocent person to sit in jail for a murder she didn't commit isn't right."

"Now, just a minute, Preacher." James W.'s eyes flashed with anger. "This is my mamma's hospital room. We're not goin' to discuss Angie's innocence—"

"Hush up, James W.," Miss Olivia interrupted, and the monitor line above her bed lurched. "Angie O'Day. You'll have to let her go."

"Why?" James W. insisted.

"You arrested the wrong person." Miss Olivia's gaze fell on Matt. "I killed Ernie Masterson."

Chapter Thirty-Three
A Matter of Duty

"Mamma, you don't know what you're sayin'," James. W. urged. He bent low over the old woman's bed. "Just because you're not doin' well, that's no reason to take the blame—"

"Hush up, James W." Miss Olivia cut him off again. "I'm too tired to argue with you. Since I'm goin' to meet my maker, I don't want this on my conscience."

"Mamma, you couldn't have lifted that crowbar if you'd wanted to," James W. argued softly. "Much less raised it up and knocked Ernie over the head with it."

"I didn't hit him with the crowbar," Miss Olivia said. "I hit him with my cane. Man deserved it, talkin' to me like that." She closed her eyes. "But he slipped on that can of soda. Went down. I hadn't meant for him to go down."

"Miss Olivia—" Elsbeth pleaded.

"Hit his head on the bumper. Hard. I knew he'd be madder than hell when he woke up. And that would be the end of it."

"End of what?" James W. asked.

"So I went up to the front of the van. The keys were in it. I turned on the ignition. He was layin' right next to the muffler. I knew it wouldn't take long."

"Mamma, why?"

"Then I went over to the wall where he keeps his tools. Turned the crowbar that matched my cane." She opened her eyes and looked at her son. "Didn't want you to think I was a murderer. It was an accident."

"Miss Olivia?" Finally Pearl spoke, and her voice could barely be heard above the monitors that blipped in the room. "You killed my husband?"

"I did you a favor," Miss Olivia said flatly. "Ernie was as bad as Cash. I was better off after Cash was dead."

"But why, Mamma?" James W. begged.

"I told you the how. I don't have to tell you the why." Miss Olivia's tone was firm. "Now I'm tired. You've got a funeral to go to." She opened her eyes and looked at Jimmy Jr. for the first time. "I'm mighty proud of you, James Wilks Novak, Jr.," she said. "You're gonna be governor."

"Miss Olivia?" Jimmy Jr. took her hand.

She closed her eyes allowing the blip on the monitor above her head to be her only reply.

"Mamma?" James W. pleaded.

Miss Olivia kept her eyes closed, her dismissal final. Slowly Elsbeth walked from the room, followed by her husband. Jimmy Jr. helped Pearl to her feet and guided her toward the door.

Matt let them pass into the hallway and took one last look

at Miss Olivia before following them. He had a sermon to give. One in which he still didn't know what he was going to say.

"Reverend Hayden?" Miss Olivia's voice was barely above a whisper.

"Yes, Miss Olivia."

"Do you know why I did it?" She half-opened her eyes.

He considered for a moment. "I imagine it's because Texas is a community property state."

She nodded her head, smiled a little, and closed her eyes.

Chapter Thirty-Four
The Preacher Has His Say

The only good thing Matt Hayden could say about his sermon was that the family was so stunned from Miss Olivia's murder confession that they probably didn't hear a word of it. Matt opened the sacristy door and hung his cross over the nail in the wardrobe, much like he'd done days earlier. Only on Wednesday, Matt had been at peace with the funeral he'd attended.

He leaned against the paneled wall. Though he'd known since midnight who had killed Ernie Masterson, it still had given him a jolt to hear it confirmed from Miss Olivia's own lips. Matt wasn't sure how he'd managed to stand before the congregation filled with members and reporters and talk for fifteen minutes about Ernie's everlasting life because of the Savior, Jesus Christ. Thinking about it now, though, Matt figured that was what divine intervention was all about.

The interment hadn't gone much easier. Ernie had been placed in a grave next to Roth and the casket for Cash Novak.

There were enough lots in the area for most of the Novak family.

But not all of them.

With a heavy sigh, Matt turned to leave the sacristy, only to see Deputy Richard Dube standing in the doorway. "Yes, Deputy?"

"The sheriff . . ." Richard cleared his throat uncomfortably. "James W. told me to come and get you."

"Me?" Matt was surprised. When he had asked James W. if he could do anything for the family, James W. flatly declined the offer. It had cut Matt to the quick.

"Yes." Deputy Dube swallowed hard, his Adam's apple bobbing wildly. "Miss Olivia is dead."

"I see," Matt said. He closed his eyes. The load of responsibility weighted down his shoulders so that he almost lost his balance.

"James W. asked if you could come straight over to the mansion. The family's gathered over there. He said to tell you he wanted some answers."

Matt nodded. James W. would naturally be angry. Wasn't it human nature to shoot the messenger? "Do me a favor, Richard," Matt said. "Swing by the Fire and Ice House and tell Dorothy Jo and Bo to come over to the mansion as well."

Richard's eyes rounded in surprise. "You want those people in Miss Olivia's mansion?" He shook his head. "There's bad blood between them and the Wilks. 'Specially now, with Angie in jail. I don't think they'll come."

"Tell 'em if they want Angie to go free, they don't have a

choice," Matt said grimly. "I'm only going to go through this once."

***

It took a full ten minutes to convince James W. to bring Angie over from the jail to sit in on the discussion they were about to have. James W. threatened Matt with charging him for withholding evidence. Matt had learned over the last week, however, that being a wimp around James W. got a person nowhere, so he stood firm, and finally James W. told Richard Dube to bring her over.

Finally, everyone was settled in the mansion's parlor. Pearl sat in the corner of the cream brocade sofa; Elsbeth in the high back upholstered chair closest. James W. leaned against one side of the mantel behind her; Jimmy Jr. rested an elbow on the other side. Dorothy Jo and Bo were in two straight back chairs brought in from the dining room.

Angie, ruffled and angry, sat at the end of a chaise across from Elsbeth, Deputy Richard Dube standing directly behind her.

"All right, Preacher, you've got us all here." James W. stood straight, hooking his thumbs authoritatively through his belt loops. "Now spill it."

Matt nodded. This would be neither pleasant, nor welcomed. So why was he going through with this?

Because the truth shall set you free, he reminded himself and smiled at Angie.

She didn't return it.

"Let's begin with the understanding that there was more than one mystery to solve here." Matt stepped forward, commanding the center of the room. "Yes, we have the mystery of who killed Ernie, but we also have a mystery concerning the whereabouts of Cash Novak, the identity of Angie's father, and the question of who murdered Maeve O'Day."

James W. growled at that last but said nothing.

"Now, why is it important to reopen the issue of Cash Novak?" Matt went on. "That happened thirty-five years ago, after all." He stopped in mid-pace. "Because for Maeve O'Day, that's where she was living." He gestured to everyone in the room. "Each one of you told me that Maeve's mind was gone with the Alzheimer's. So how do we know that she was living thirty-five years ago?" He looked around the room, but no one answered.

"Because one of the last things she said that you remembered, Angie, was that she had called someone on the television J.J." He turned to Jimmy Jr. "In her mind, you were J.J."

"No one's ever called me that." Jimmy Jr. looked puzzled.

"No," Matt agreed, "but you look like someone, call it hereditary, that Maeve once called J.J." He looked at Dorothy Jo. "Doesn't he?"

Dorothy Jo blushed crimson as all eyes in the room turned on her. She shook her head.

"Dorothy Jo, they're all dead now. You're the only one left who knows the truth," Matt said gently. "I'll help you. Cash Novak's real name was James Johann Novak."

Elsbeth gasped. "J.J.," she whispered.

Dorothy Jo bowed her head. "They were in love. Cash and Maeve. They met one night when Cash came over to have a good time with the . . . paid help." She stammered, "Maeve was new at Miss Lida's. Maeve poured him a tequila and that was it. He never left the bar the whole night. Never slept with any of the girls after that either."

She looked up at Matt and he nodded for her to continue.

"Cash was real in love with his first wife, Roth's mother. He married Miss Olivia because his family wanted it." She hefted out a breath. "He'd already re-enlisted to serve in Viet Nam. I think he was hopin' he wouldn't come back alive, and he wanted Roth cared for, so he agreed to the marriage."

"But he did come back," Matt said.

"Miss Olivia wasn't real happy about it, neither." Dorothy Jo's voice was filled with disdain. "Got pregnant with James W. and never slept with him again. Cash Novak had been a lonely man for a lotta years."

"Then he met Maeve O'Day."

Dorothy Jo nodded. "I think she reminded him of his first wife. Full of spunk, Maeve always was, and a good listener. And she was beautiful."

Angie let out a whimper, and Matt realized her face was streaked with tears. "Are you sayin' that Cash Novak was my father?"

Dorothy Jo lowered her head. "Before you were ever born I promised your mamma I'd keep her secret. I didn't know you then, but since you've grown up, there hasn't been a day gone by that I haven't regretted makin' that promise. But you know your mamma. I couldn't break it, not then, and not now, though she's gone."

Angie nodded. Maeve O'Day held a standard on promises that couldn't be compromised. If Dorothy Jo had broken it, Maeve would never have forgiven her. Even from the grave.

"Cash Novak was Angie's father." The whispered statement cut into the room like a knife, and all eyes turned on Elsbeth.

"That's right," Matt nodded. Elsbeth rested her head in her hands and began sobbing quietly.

"Okay, my dad fathered her." James W. was still angry. "What does that have to do with Ernie?"

"Pearl, you'll have to pardon me speaking this way." Matt looked apologetically toward the new widow.

Pearl nodded. "Go on, Pastor. Nobody knows more than I do that he wasn't perfect."

"Ernie Masterson was an opportunist." Matt's tone was grim. "The night the news came about Roth's death, Ernie was given the opportunity of a lifetime."

"Why?" Pearl asked.

Matt took a deep breath. "Because he already knew by that time that Cash Novak was dead."

Chapter Thirty-Five
A Sad Love Story

Pastor Matt Hayden held up his hands to still the din that had taken over the parlor. "Yes, I know Cash had been seen in Houston for the Reagan debate. He'd made sure he had witnesses, 'cuz he wanted an alibi that was firm."

"Alibi for what?"

"For spending time with the new love in his life. Maeve O'Day. The only one whose word we had that Cash was actually in Houston for *all three* days was Ernie's. My guess is that Ernie's cabin was where they spent their time together. It was certainly out in the middle of nowhere."

Slowly the heads in the room began to nod as they realized it was true.

Matt continued. "I suspect Cash Novak died in Maeve O'Day's arms at Ernie's cabin. Call it a heart attack, stroke, I have no idea. But the only thing Maeve knew to do was call Ernie Masterson, 'cuz Ernie was probably the only one who knew that Cash and Maeve were at his place."

Dorothy Jo sobbed into her handkerchief, the small nod of her head the only confirmation Matt needed to go on. "Ernie didn't know what to do, but he knew he had to get Maeve out of there. He drove her back to Miss Lida's hotel—" Matt flashed a look in Elsbeth's direction, "—suitcase and all."

"Where did Ernie go then?" James W. asked.

"It's a guess," Matt continued, "but I think Ernie came here to the mansion and told Miss Olivia what had happened. He knew that Miss Olivia would not want it known where, or with whom, Cash had really died, so they had to come up with a plan to dispose of Cash's body. A very lucrative plan for Ernie, I'm sure."

"Cash was dead before Roth? And Miss Olivia knew it?" Elsbeth asked in horror.

"It's a guess, but I'll bet money on it," Matt said. "When Pastor Osterburg came here the next day to tell Miss Olivia of Roth's death, she was already wearing black. Pastor Osterburg also said that Miss Olivia was silent for a whole five minutes after she'd been given the news of Roth's death. He timed it." Matt pointed to the wind-up clock that still ticked on the mantel.

"That would have been enough time for her to have done a lot of thinking. And worrying."

"Worryin' about what?" James W. asked.

Matt looked kindly at Pearl, and she nodded for him to continue. He could see in her gaze that she'd already guessed the truth.

"Worrying that if Cash was declared dead before Roth,

Roth's widow stood to inherit Wilks property as well as Novak."

Pearl closed her eyes.

"Texas is a community property state. There was a written agreement that joined the Wilks and Novak properties on the date of Miss Olivia and Cash's wedding. If Cash preceded either Roth or James W. in death, not only Novak property, but also Wilks property would be split with the descendants. That probably seemed incredibly unfair to Miss Olivia, since Roth didn't have a drop of Wilks blood in him. Every bit of Wilks property, in her mind, should have gone only to James W. It rankled Miss Olivia that Roth's wife should have any claim on the Wilks name."

"Wilks blood was always so important to her," Elsbeth said quietly. "I'm Wilks from a third cousin. Be honest, James W. She picked me for you."

"There're other things I love about you." James W.'s voice was hoarse.

"So it was important to Miss Olivia that Roth's death be claimed *before* Cash's. That way everything she had could go to James W. and her blood alone," said Matt.

"She probably could have fought the community property issue in court, if she'd wanted to," Jimmy Jr. offered.

"In 1980? The mind-set of the country was different back then. You didn't go to court, especially grieving widows," Matt returned. "It was much easier simply to adjust the time of Cash's death to erase any question. After all, both Roth and Cash were dead, so why not fix everything the easy way? But it wasn't easy. She needed Ernie to get rid of Cash's body, and to tell the lie that Cash had been alive and well in Houston when Roth died. And Ernie exacted his price."

"Pearl," Bo finally spoke.

"Pearl." Matt confirmed. "Plus a good portion of the Novak land. Especially the acreage where Cash's body had been hidden."

James W. shook his head. "Miss Olivia and Ernie knew where Cash was, all that time we looked for him?"

"Ernie put him there," Matt said. "But in all honesty, most of Cash's remains probably didn't last very long."

"Where was he?" James W. demanded.

"Disintegrated, I should imagine, from the bacteria." Matt said. He looked straight at Elsbeth. "Dumped in the outhouse behind Cash's old cabin."

"The toilet paper," Elsbeth whispered.

"Maeve O'Day knew exactly what had happened to the man she loved," Matt said. "You were right; she wanted money from Miss Olivia to keep her secret. Apparently she got it, and a few other things, as well."

"Other things?" Angie asked.

"The liquor license for the Fire and Ice House. The only way that could've gotten through the town council was if Miss Olivia let it be known that no one was to fight it. I don't think Maeve considered it blackmail, exactly. Maybe she thought she had the right to make a living to raise Cash's child." He turned to Jimmy Jr. "If Maeve had pressed for it in the courts, she probably could have gotten a great deal more than she asked for from Miss Olivia."

"For her part, Maeve kept her mouth shut," Dorothy Jo said. "She kept her word better'n any Wilks ever has."

James W. stepped forward angrily. "My father was buried in a pile of—?"

"I'm sure Miss Olivia saw some sort of justice in that, don't you think?" Matt shook his head. "Everything she did was logical. Not terribly kind. Certainly not loving. But it was logical."

"What happened to my mother?" Angie demanded.

Matt blew out a deep sigh. "Now to the present. Only the present for Maeve O'Day was the past. When she saw Jimmy Jr. on TV, to Maeve's confused mind, she was looking at J.J., *her* name for Cash Novak. Remember, 'Cash' was only a nickname. His real name was James Johann Novak. J.J. He must've loved Maeve a great deal to reveal to her what his true name was. And to Maeve, Cash was not a scoundrel, but a sad, lonely widower in a loveless marriage of convenience. Cash was the man the world knew. J.J. was the man she loved. When she saw Jimmy Jr., the spitting image of Cash Novak, it took her back to a time when she was in love and young and beautiful. Back to a time before she'd made promises to keep quiet about her love. When Maeve went out for her walk that day, she asked everyone if they'd seen her J.J. They passed off her question as the ravings of an Alzheimer's victim. Everyone except the one person who knew who J.J. was."

"Miss Olivia," Dorothy Jo supplied, piecing it together as Matt spoke. "Cash and Miss Olivia argued about Maeve more than once. He wanted a divorce, you know."

"So when Miss Olivia heard that Maeve O'Day was asking about J.J., she realized that all the lies of the past three decades were unravelling around her. Just when all of her work at being silent was finally coming to fruition."

Pearl spoke up. "She might've heard me and Ernie talking about Maeve asking around town about a J.J. person. Someone had pulled up to the garage, but then left in an awful hurry before Ernie could get out there. And Miss Olivia was scheduled to have her car worked on that afternoon."

"That would make sense," Matt agreed.

"What do you mean all of her silence was coming to fruition?" Elsbeth asked.

Matt shifted his gaze to Jimmy Jr. "Her grandson was running for governor of Texas."

Jimmy Jr. paled, but Matt knew he had to finish what he'd started.

"So Miss Olivia coaxed Maeve and Shadow into her car. She gave Shadow some meat mixed with poison from her gardening shed so that he couldn't lead Maeve back to town. Then Miss Olivia drove Maeve and Shadow out to the deer lease where she knew a stupid Yankee was hunting with a gun he didn't know how to use."

Matt turned toward James W. "I'm not sure she really wanted to kill Maeve O'Day. But she wanted to get rid of her. Perhaps confuse her so bad she wouldn't remember *anything*. Every one of you said Maeve was very frail. All Miss Olivia had to do was make her sick enough to forget everything. Even J.J. From Miss Olivia's point of view, what better place for Maeve

O'Day to be than on the same property where Cash had died in her arms."

"Then things turned sour." Matt shook his head. "Because Ernie knew exactly who had driven Maeve O'Day out of town. That afternoon he cleaned out Miss Olivia's car and he probably found Shadow's dog hair in the back seat, or maybe he'd even witnessed Miss Olivia driving Maeve out of town. Remember how he pointed out the black dog hair in the back of her car? Blanco's fur is white. However it came to be that Ernie learned of Miss Olivia's involvement, don't forget, he was ever the opportunist."

The room was silent as he drank down a glass of water. "So that night, when Elsbeth was looking for Ernie, Miss Olivia knew she had to do something to keep Ernie's silence. She went over to the garage, but Elsbeth had gotten there before her. Elsbeth didn't hear Miss Olivia enter through the office because of the storm. From what Miss Olivia heard Ernie say to Elsbeth, however, she knew that she would have to meet Ernie's price for silence yet again. If his price wasn't met, Ernie might call Elsbeth, or worse, the newspapers, and spill everything. Miss Olivia's world was falling apart."

James W. brought his head up sharply. "Elsbeth, you saw Ernie on Wednesday night?"

Elsbeth glared at the preacher.

"James W., Ernie caused a lot of trouble in his lifetime," Matt said. "Don't keep it going now."

"Ernie brought it on himself," Pearl said quietly. "I'm glad he's dead."

Elsbeth sighed. "Now, honey,"

"I can't believe I cried so hard for him that night," Pearl said. She looked at Bo. "You let me. You held my hand and let me."

"When?" James W. asked.

"Wednesday night. After you and Reverend Hayden came over. I went to the Fire and Ice House." She swallowed hard. "Bo knew how Ernie treated me. The night before, they even got in a fight about it."

"That's how the black bandanna came to be in your possession," James W. said.

"There was a scuffle." Pearl nodded. "I'd forgotten I even had it until I went to fold it."

James W. turned on Richard Dube. "I thought you were watchin' the house and the garage Wednesday night."

"I did," Richard said, his Adam's apple bobbing wildly. "I told you. Not a soul came near the place."

"Pearl's sayin' she went over to the Ice House."

"Sure. She left about fifteen minutes after you and the preacher."

James W.'s mouth opened, then shut again. "Why didn't you tell me?"

"I thought you wanted to know if somebody *came* to the gas station." Richard's eyes lit with excitement. "You know, the murderer returnin' to the scene of the crime."

James W. bowed his head, and Matt could see he was biting back several epitaphs.

"What I do with my time and with whom I choose to spend it is none of your business anyway, James W." Pearl's voice was quiet, but firm. "All these years I've been married to a man who didn't love me, and whom I didn't love." She looked at Bo and smiled. "It's my turn to be happy, James W. So stay out of it."

"Miss Olivia really did kill Ernie," Elsbeth said in a hushed voice.

"Yes," Matt said. "Probably exactly the way James W. had it figured. When I went to walk Blanco Thursday morning, it didn't strike me at the time, but Miss Olivia's gloves, scarf, and coat were all wet. The only way that could've happened was if she'd gone out in the storm the night before."

There was a long silence in the room, save for the quiet sobs of Dorothy Jo. Finally a stricken Elsbeth spoke. "So what do we do now, Pastor?"

"My answer is easy, but you're carrying it out will be very difficult, I'm afraid." Matt looked directly at Angie, then James W. "You've all been wronged, one way or another. You've been lied to, used, kept from learning truths you deserved to know."

"What are you suggesting?" James W. asked.

"Make right what's been done wrong. Give the respect—and the assets—each one of you is due." He let out a small chuckle. "All you have to do is love each other."

"My mother's dyin' today . . . did we cause it by stirring her all up this morning?" James W.'s eyes filled with tears.

"No," Matt replied. "I imagine Miss Olivia simply did what she thought was her duty."

Chapter Thirty-Six
Gettin' Out of Dodge

It was a week after Miss Olivia's death, and Matt had seen little of the Wilks clan except for their matriarch's funeral. His offers to help them through the rough time had been politely, but firmly, refused. So, for the fifth night in a row, Matt sat alone in his front room. The parsonage lights were out, the hearth dark. Earlier, in a restless mood, he'd unpacked a few boxes and hung a few pictures. Now he gave in to the melancholy that tore at him.

He should go to see her.

He couldn't go to see her.

She was everything he wanted.

She was the only person he could not have.

The knock at the door jolted him from his thoughts, and he pulled himself to his feet. He was in no mood for company, but an interruption might be what he needed.

He pulled open the door. "Angie."

"Hey, Preacher."

Matt swallowed. Her hair fell in glowing copper waves under the moonlight.

"You really are beautiful." He realized seconds later he had put his thoughts into words.

"You're not so bad yourself." Angie's voice was low. Husky. Perfect, like the rest of her.

Matt pulled himself together. He'd been thinking of her, dreaming of her. This was no dream, however. Reality stood like a brick wall between them. He knew he should ask her to come in. He desperately wanted to ask her. However, he couldn't trust himself for what might happen when the door closed.

As if reading his thoughts, Angie took his hand and pulled him inside the house. "We won't shut the door, all right?"

"All right," he said, even though he shivered against the wind.

"You wanna get a jacket or something?"

"You still have my coat," he reminded her. "So what's on your mind, Angie?"

She leaned back against the open door. "Thanks for gettin' me out," she said.

Matt nodded. "You trusted me."

"You came through." Angie folded her arms across her chest. "Now I need you to trust me."

Matt knew his look was defensive.

"Not so easy, is it?" she chuckled.

"No. Especially when I find I can't trust myself."

Angie nodded her head in understanding. "That's part of

the problem. Your problem, I mean. You've always been so sure of yourself. Now the very thing you know you want is the one thing you shouldn't want. It shakes your confidence, doesn't it?"

"You came here to talk about my problems?" Matt asked.

"No. I came to talk about our problem." Her smile turned sad. "Us. I came to talk about us."

Matt sighed. "Can there be an 'us'?"

"That's the problem. Take my hand, Preacher."

He did as she bid, and the simple touch sent a jolt all the way up his arm to his heart.

"There *is* an us," she whispered.

"Yes." He knew it. Had known it. "Yes, there is. But I don't want to hurt you, Angie."

"And I'm not in the mood to be hurt. So that's what I'm here to say. But you've gotta trust me, like I trusted you."

"What exactly am I supposed to trust you about?"

"I'm goin' away."

"What?" He stood straighter. "Where?"

"Ireland."

"Why?"

"Because I have family there. James W. is making good on givin' Pearl and me Novak money. I've always wanted to know my mamma's people."

Matt studied her face in the moonlight. Only now was he able to take the time to see how her nose turned up slightly at its tip and that her neck was longer than he'd remembered. "I'm chasing you away."

She smiled. "No. You're the reason I'm comin' back."

"When?"

"When enough time has passed." She grinned. "Besides, you have some mysteries I want to solve."

"Like what?"

"Like how when we were lookin' for my mamma you said your brother was a cop in Denver, and then when we're in front of a fire, he's a cop in Florida. You don't talk about your past, which for a man of the cloth is downright sacrilegious. You've got secrets, Preacher. I aim to find 'em out."

"Then what?"

She grinned. Shrugged. Matt knew he was in for a heap of trouble with that look. "So this is a done deal," he said.

"I got it all worked out. James W.'s gonna take Shadow. Dorothy Jo and Bo'll keep the Ice House open." Her eyes twinkled. "I'm gonna let you use my truck. James W. said your car's a lemon."

"He did, did he?"

"I figure you'd rather have my truck than Miss Olivia's car."

This time Matt laughed. "You're right." He sobered. "When do you leave?"

"As soon as I can get a passport. They can do somethin' they call 'expedite' it nowadays."

He nodded. So she would be gone soon, and for quite a while. Already he was beginning to feel empty inside.

Angie smiled. "You're sad."

Matt took both of her hands in his. "Yes." Her hands were soft but strong, he thought, just like the woman who stood before him. He pulled her hands to his lips, kissed them gently, and was surprised to see her cheeks grow pink in the moonlight. "And you're shy," he said with a grin. He turned thoughtful. "There is a lot we have to learn about each other."

"That's what makes fallin' in love so much fun."

Love.

Well, if she could be strong enough, so could he. Matt stood a little straighter. "Okay. There are two things I need before you leave." He put his hand to her cheek and tipped her chin towards him. "First." Leaning in, looking first into her eyes and then for her lips, he gently kissed her.

Soft. Innocent. Then, not so innocent. When he pulled back, both of them took a long moment to bring their breathing back under control.

"You said two things?" Angie finally asked, her voice barely a whisper.

He let his smile come slowly. "I appreciate that you're taking care of me—giving me time to work this all out, letting me use your truck and all, but there's something else I need."

She apparently caught on that he was teasing because Angie put her hand to her hip and placed a come-hither look on her face. "What else can I do for you, preacher man?"

He arched his brow and slowly leaned in toward her, this time putting his lips at her ear, making sure his breath tickled her skin. "Before you go," he whispered.

"Yes?" she breathed back.

"Can I please have my coat back?"

At least this time her punch to his stomach didn't knock the breath out of him. Grinning, she tossed the coat over his shoulder, then headed back toward her side of the river. The wind whipped at her hair and her stride showed just enough sass, he noted, unable to look away. As she was about to cross the Mason Street Bridge, she turned. "Wanted to make sure you didn't forget me, preacher!"

"Oh, Lord." He looked heavenward. "I thought you put me here to keep me out of trouble."

Coming in November, 2016

Murder in the Second Pew

next in the Preacher Matt Hayden Mystery Series.

Acknowledgments

"Write what you know" is excellent advice. I thank the following folks for allowing me to learn from them and be inspired by them.

Dad, you were a wonderful preacher. Give my love to mom up there in heaven.

On a completely different note, I thank all my friends at Backspin in Austin, Texas, especially Brooke, Dawn and Diana. None of you are redheads (most of the time), but you all had a hand in Angie. And of course, thanks Robert, the man with the long ponytail, who is a fount of interesting experiences.

I am grateful to the Smith Point Writer's Group of Houston, Texas. Your critiques and encouragement have allowed this book to become reality.

Ann, Anne Marie, Kay, the Other Kay, and Terri—you guys are the best. I am grateful to you and our beloved mentor, BK Reeves, for the overnight critique sessions, weekly get-togethers and incredible support.

To Regina Morris and Silkhaven Publishing, thank you for you for all of your efforts and support. You are amazing.

Finally, to my husband and daughter. I am so glad you both are patient, pushy and sometimes believe more in my writing than I do. Let's keep on laughing!

About the Author

K.P. Gresham enjoys writing humorous cozy mysteries as well as audacious (in all its definitions) mainstream novels. Due to her quirky fixation with adventure plus the fascinating inspirations provided by members of the human race, K.P. has a never-ending source of story lines and characters. For the Preacher Matt Hayden Mystery Series, K.P. grew up as a "Preacher's Kid" in Illinois, then married an awesome guy who whisked her away to a paradise called Texas. Both experiences put the truth into her fictional and beloved Grace Lutheran Church of Wilks, Texas. A graduate of Illinois State University and a middle school literature teacher for many years (again, lots of fodder for lots of tales), writing humorous mysteries combines her lifelong love of laughing, reading and enjoying a great whodunit.

Besides mysteries, K.P. also writes mainstream fiction. *Three Days at Wrigley Field* revolves around her life-long loyalty to the Chicago Cubs. In this novel K.P. explores the ends to which the Cubs' owner will go in order to win the ever ever-out-of-reach World Series. His solution is a "Rembrandt" of a closing pitcher. Who happens to be a woman. (You were warned that it was audacious.)

K.P.'s moniker is "have story, will write," and she hasn't stopped writing for over fifty years! Visit her at www.kpgresham.com.

Also available from
K.P.Gresham

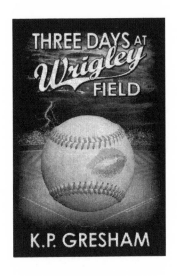

Available on Amazon
and Barnes and Noble or visit her website at
www.kpgresham.com

Made in the USA
Middletown, DE
24 January 2022

58416446R00149